Prologue

The Denver Post - December

Boulder County's First Hydraulic Fracturing Well Site Destroyed in Fiery Explosion

The FBI is offering a $750,000 reward for information leading to the arrest of an unknown number of suspects in the explosion of a large hydraulic fracturing drilling site in Boulder County, Colorado. No deaths or injuries have been reported. According to statements from the Boulder County Sheriff's Department, multiple local, state and federal agencies cooperated in fire suppression and are working together in the investigation. Authorities have asked that witnesses with information please contact the Boulder County Sheriff's Department or FBI field office in Denver. The site was the first to be drilled after county commissioners lifted the moratorium on hydraulic fracturing applications in Boulder County Open Spaces.

Investigators have determined that a diesel pickup truck was driven at high speed directly into the wellhead and drill tower, causing a large explosion heard by witnesses as far as 20 miles away. Firefighting crews were unable to extinguish the flames, some reaching 150 feet into the air, for nearly two days. The fiery inferno was not extinguished until specialty teams from Texas arrived with explosives designed to suffocate wellhead blazes. Little remains of the truck that was driven into the drill tower, and investigators have not determined the type of explosive material used in the blast.

State authorities have determined that the owner of the truck used to blow up the fracking site is Mr. Keith Sutton of Greeley. Sutton is the mayor of Greeley and also the current chairman of the Colorado Oil and Gas Conservation Commission. Mr. Sutton claims that he and his wife were leaving a party in Boulder (ironically they were celebrating the first drill site on Boulder public lands) when his truck was stolen.

The commissioner reported that an unknown voice came over the vehicle's sound system and commanded them to exit their vehicle before it detonated at the conclusion of a ten second countdown. The voice began counting down through the truck's sound system, and the couple fled the vehicle for their lives. Both claim that the truck drove off without a driver at the wheel and that the stereo system was blaring loud music. The commissioner's wife, Mrs. Tamara (Tam) Sutton, who is also the president of the University of Northern Colorado, declined any further comment.

The Boulder County Sheriff's Department said in a press conference yesterday that a lack of evidence continues to hamper the investigation. The magnitude of the wellhead explosion and the ensuing fire left little of the truck intact; parts of the vehicle were found as far as 300 meters away.

A first-responder photograph taken approximately 12 minutes after the explosion was analyzed to determine the vehicle's license plate number and owner. Investigators have revealed that the letters *ADOG* were crudely written on the grime-covered license plate. Officials believe the culprit(s) may have written the word on the license plate before the truck was driven at high speed into the wellhead.

Over the course of the 46 hour battle with the raging fire, the letters could not be distinguished any longer due to the intense heat, the high volume of flame retardant, and the last explosion used to suffocate the fire at the wellhead. Investigators could not confirm that the word *ADOG* on the license plate might be related to the suspect(s), to Mr. Sutton, or any of his associates.

If you have any information related to the bombing of the Boulder County wellhead facility, please contact the Boulder County Sheriff's Department or FBI field office in Denver.

Yes, it's true, we blew it sky high.

Miles away, in a dimly-lit office at the Engineering Center at the University of Colorado, three graduate students clinked open Odell's IPA bottles as Big Head Todd and the Monsters wailed the John Lee Hooker song, *Boom Boom*. They had successfully hijacked the commissioner's truck by remote control.

The driverless truck travelled unnoticed to its designated rendezvous with their mercenary friend three miles from wellhead. He filled the truck with explosives before grinning and inscribing "ADOG" across the dirt-encrusted license plate.

The truck's speedometer reading at the time of impact was approximately twice the speed of a hound, or about 84 miles per hour. They never saw, heard or felt the ferocity of the fiery explosion from the safety of their professor's office where they danced euphorically to the music, pumping their fists, unable to contain their glee:

Boom Boom Boom Boom!
Bang Bang Bang Bang!
I'm gonna shoot you right down
Right offa your feet

A-Haw Haw Haw Haw!

Not exactly the stuff of puppy play: blowing up the first drilling site on Boulder County Open Space. What could possibly motivate these young men to commit themselves to such a high standard of duty in public service and community outreach?

Good question. I just as well tell you the reasons.

Chapter 1 – Will's Trifecta

Do you remember hearing my voice for the first time?

Maybe you didn't recognize it when you were younger. Or maybe you did and chose to ignore it or confused it for the voice of another. It's also possible that you and I converse with some frequency on many matters, or just a few. I use the word *converse* loosely here, and elsewhere, since my conversations are mostly one-way. Outside of fielding good questions, I do the majority of the talking, and you do the majority of the listening.

It's simply how it works. And I realize that you're a homo sapien, but there is no need to feel either proud or picked upon because of it. I've been in this line of work with numerous other species for far longer than your kind has been roaming and ravaging that still-beautiful planet of yours. For the sake of understanding me and the sort of beings that listen to my voice, let us first consider the characters in the mysterious picture that is the focus of this book.

You may have seen it before, and you might even recognize some of the faces, but too few know what really happened that semester.

It begins on the Colorado Front Range with a mountain lion listening intently to me near the base of Storm Mountain, just beyond Loveland, Colorado. Yes, it's true. I helped her kill Will Fiedler's dog Kota, a golden retriever mix he'd had since he was 14.

I also use the word *helped* loosely here; she was already an adept predator: patient, good at concealing herself, and a solid judge of sprint distances. In matters involving the quick and efficient death of her prey, she is a master worthy of emulation.

Sniffing and running carefree off-trail after rabbits and squirrels, Kota never saw the big cat waiting patiently in the tree on the edge of Jug Trail that late afternoon in August. It's also true that I told Will more than once that hiking a dog off leash in the wilds of Colorado comes with risks. And that I am always happy to discuss them— helping you assess risk is a large part of my work.

On this particular occasion at the base of Storm Mountain, it was too late for me to help Will. He heard the loud wails of his dog and the sounds of a scuffle on loose rocks near a tall pine. By the time he saw them, the lion already had Kota by the small of the back, and she struggled to turn, snarl and bite at the large predator between squalls and human-like screams that pierced the quietude of the side canyon.

Will raced toward the struggling animals at full speed over the uneven rocky ground, shouting and cursing wildly at the top of his voice. He stooped twice in his sprint to grab any rocks of throwing size, which he hurled with all his might at the predator. He was still too far away; the stones fell short. I advised him to sprint, which he did, but for just long enough to trip and perform a near-flawless face plant. He barely registered the searing burn of skin peeling off his left shin and the penetration of sharp granite rocks into his thigh, stomach and hands as he tried to break the fall.

Will looked up, spitting sand and grit, to see the lion press Kota's small frame to the ground before doubling down with powerful jaws into her neck.

He picked himself up, and instead of throwing rocks, he hurled guttural obscenities and waved his arms wildly, running directly at the predator and her prey. Kota's howling and snarling for mercy became muffled and gurgled, and Will could see between his swelling tears that her body had ceased resistance and gone limp.

Will ran faster and screamed louder, but the lion quickly re-applied her powerful jaws to the back of Kota's neck,

8

picked her up, and swiftly bounded up onto a rock ledge and into the cover of the large boulders.

When Will reached the base of the rocks, I mentioned that following a lion into its territory comes with risks that are complicated, especially when food is involved. Panting heavily, he looked up the steepening incline patched with wax currant bushes and occasionally obscured by the enormous boulders. Will's tears and confusion turned to anger when I spoke, as flatly and softly as I do, to explain what had just occurred to them.

Will stiffened up straight and curled his hands into tight fists. He could feel adrenaline burn through his veins as he threw his head back and howled with searing rage at the ambivalent blue sky and tan-gray ridgelines. Will howled until his throat became dry and hoarse, but it was moistened soon after, as he wept bitterly on his knees with his head in his hands. He is not the first of your kind I've heard wailing with regret for not listening to me, and trust me, he won't be the last.

Will returned to the Jug Trail side canyon well before midnight. Parking with an open view of the ridge line from the driver's side, he rolled down the window and listened quietly in the star-speckled August night. With a far-reaching flashlight and his dad's 12 gauge shotgun, Will dozed in, but mostly out, of sporadic sleep, dreaming of the lion caching a lifeless and half-eaten Kota somewhere up there on the lonely mountain.

The howls of the coyotes jolted Will from his intermittent snoozing. Their yips and chortles permeated the early morning like a drunken party of rowdy ruffians. Will immediately stepped out of his truck and pumped the shotgun, firing two shells into the emptiness of the night sky where he could see the long, bright fiery fingers boom towards the cursed ridgeline.

Will trained his flashlight onto the boulders and looked keenly for any telltale signs of light reflecting from the eyes of an animal.

Nothing.

He spent most of the remaining dark hours of the early morning turning on and turning off the light. He saw no reflections except for small pieces of mica glittering in the rocks and dirt of the side canyon.

When the new day shed its first light on the ridgeline, Will hiked back to the boulders, heavy with anger and sorrow, having no hope of finding Kota or her remains. Yes, I convinced him there was no hope of finding her, and I was correct. She was gone.

But Will's courage and tenacity did not go unnoticed, and partially explains why I am telling you this story about another fight against some other very big cats. Regardless of my explanations and your emotions, have you ever noticed that among your kind, hardships often come in threes? We could call them trifectas, and in this, our story, it was Will's turn for one.

Go Number 2

Since Will began listening to me at an early age, he became adept at math, science and technology. The son of an electrician, he learned quickly to understand power, design-documents, equipment and technologies for engineers. He spent four years at Colorado State University in Fort Collins for a degree in engineering and was embarking on his second year as a graduate student in Aerospace Engineering at the University of Colorado in Boulder (CU).

Yes, the mighty Republic of Boulder, Colorado, where nearly everyone has a cause and most appreciate the goodness of craft beer, dogs, cannabis and the outdoors. As you might imagine, this setting is ideal; many of my very best conversations have occurred in the outdoors.

It was the middle of August and the start of the fall semester at CU, when Will carried the hole in his soul for his dog back to Boulder. He had left his family's home in Masonville and was thinking about his parents, their financial worries, and how they would adapt to them when his phone rang. It was Aldo, his roommate.

"Hey man, I've got some bad news," Aldo said.

Will paused.

"How about the good news first?"

There was no good news. Will and Aldo had rented a house for the academic year, but the house had been sold, and the new owners were renovating, not renting. Regardless of my involvement in the sale of their rental house in Boulder, they were in a predicament in a housing market reflective of the mighty Republic's wealth, livability and construction moratoriums.

Will decided to sleep in the back of his truck that night parked at Lost Gulch, along Boulder Creek. Early the following morning, he scrambled out of his sleeping bag and camper-topped truck and headed to his office cubicle in the Engineering Center on CU's campus. Will was scrolling through apartment listings when he suddenly heard the sound of running footsteps and a man shouting, "I found it! I found it!"

Will heard the running feet come to a sliding stop in front of another professor's office. Seeing no one there, the running man sprinted back down the hall and came to a squeaking, skidding stop in front of the graduate student office doorway.

"Dr. Schwede!" Will said putting on his best grin for his major professor. Schwede resembled a medieval monk. Barefoot and balding with a fringe of dark hair, he brimmed with brilliance, and his eyes burned with the intensity of an obsessive problem solver. Dr. Schwede and I have actually conversed a great deal, and he is a master listener, especially in the realm of physics and modern weaponry.

"I found the answer for the stealth battleship displacement tonnage!" Schwede said excitedly flipping his tablet around to show Will a mass of complex formulas in the language of fluid dynamics and composite materials. Assisted by his graduate students, Will and Aldo, the renowned CU professor was nearing completion on two major

Department of Defense contracts for the US Navy and US
Air Force.

The Charming Third

Despite their best efforts searching, Will and Aldo were
unable to find an apartment, but they did find good beer
and food at The West End Tavern on the Pearl Street Mall
in Boulder. They were seated at the bar discussing together
with me the next steps in their living situation when a tall,
lean and balding bearded man entered the bar with a dog.
Hearing the sound of ticking toe claws on the tavern floor,
Will turned to see the man and the hound-mix approaching
the empty seat next to him.

Will slid off his bar stool and bent smiling with the back of
his hand extended to the nearly all-white hound with the
brown and black mask. The dog stopped momentarily and
locked eyes with Will while she and I went through the
usual checklist of odors and energies for discerning good
from bad men.

Proceeding to him, the hound dog sat up and balanced
herself on her haunches. From this position, she extended
her right front paw in the air towards Will, who stuck out

14

his hand and caught it neatly in his palm. The hound looked again into Will's eyes before she reached up to touch her soft wet black nose to Will's nose. After sniffing him for a moment, the dog ended with one big lick starting from the middle of his chin and ending at the tip of his nose.

"That's Pearly," said the sturdy, lean man with a grin, "and a solid judge of character."

Will and Aldo looked up at the bearded man. He was clad in a worn, torn and unbuttoned collared shirt that matched his grubby shorts. He had unusually bright eyes that shimmered in the multiverse of the half-lit tavern like the eyes of some mythical wild canine. Will thought that he recognized him, but his sleep-deprived brain and sorrow-riddled emotions worked against his best recollections and me.

Aldo was taking his turn to rub Pearly's neck and scratch her back when the bearded man sat down on the barstool next to them and put an outdated, worn and heavy leather wallet onto the bar. At his request, the bartender poured the man a Melvin IPA, from which he took a slow and savory swallow before letting out an audible, "Mmmmm."

"Dowg!" shouted a short man with a large, nearly perfectly round beer belly at the end of the bar. "What are you doing here drinking alcohol?"

"Would you ask me a similar question if you saw me getting my hair cut at the barbershop?" the scruffy man questioned dryly. Pearly lifted her head and shot him a quick glance. Attempting to hide their chuckles, Will took another sip of his Liquid Mechanics Hop Nectar, and Aldo shifted his attention to the large TV screen that dominated the wall in front of him. On it, the evening news appeared briefly between long and severe bouts of commercials.

The beer-bellied man continued his questioning from across the bar in a loud, half-drunk, fully obnoxious voice. "Shouldn't you be at some dirty place of ill-repute, Dowg? You hypocrite!"

Will took another tug of beer, set it down and stared into the half-empty pub glass. Aldo turned again to look at the TV on the opposite end of the bar. Neither were sure if the potbellied man and the ragged stranger bantering at the bar were having fun or about to have words.

"How is it that the sun visits cesspools, and even the top of your hollow head, yet the sun is not defiled?" the man called Dowg retorted. He took another savory swallow of beer and looked up at the incessant stimulation of the TV screen to ignore the potbellied heckler. A vacant-eyed, perfectly-coiffed blonde was just beginning a "special report."

"A Masonville, Colorado man has bulldozed his home to the ground in response to a feud with Wells Fargo Bank," the newscaster read from her script in front of a full-screen photograph of the man on the TV. "The man claims that the bank repossessed his house when he missed his last mortgage payment despite having paid off all but $20,000 of the $300,000 debt. The homeowner, Guy Fiedler, an electrician, attributed heavy business losses over the last two years to the missed payments."

"Fiedler claims that the banks and mortgage holders have no right to possess his house," the newscaster read from the prompter. The TV footage of the aftermath showed that the house had been pushed into a large, nearly flattened mound that began in the bottom of the swimming pool.

"Bravo!" exclaimed Dowg with delight, laughter and loud applause as he watched the TV. *"Now there's an honest man!"*

Will was glued to the TV, staring speechlessly. Dowg continued clapping loudly, and Aldo squinted to look more closely at the picture of the man on the TV and the footage of the bulldozed wreckage of the home. "Hey dude, that looks a hell'uva a lot like your dad! Is that your house?"

Dowg glanced over at Will and noticed that he seemed to be on the verge of tears or laughter or both.

Yes, it's true. I convinced Guy Fiedler to demolish their home, and as the owner of an electrical company, he was familiar with heavy equipment and did a fine job of it. In our conversation together, we concluded that it was mostly math in dollars—if we lose big—so does the bank. I do recall Mr. Fiedler concluding our conversation with a string of creative and colorful curses before he started up the bulldozer, lifted the large metal blade and put it into gear.

Trifecta worry was written all over Will's face, body and spirit. He turned his device on to call his mother, and the ping of a new message showed that she had already called.

"Will, your dad's lost his mind! Have you seen the news? He bulldozed the house! Our house! He put all our stuff in the shop. He may end up in jail! I'll call you from granny's when I get there. I'm fine, try not to worry."

Will pictured his mom's anxious face, and their possessions stuffed into a service-truck bay at *Fiedler Electric*. He pictured his dad sitting at the shop with a shotgun across his lap, keeping his eyes peeled for any Wells Fargo attorneys.

Aldo ordered Will a shot of tequila and filled Dowg in on Will's recent spate of outcomes. Observing the tones of their voices and body language, Pearly was compelled to display affection for Will. Again, she balanced herself on her haunches and pawed at his thigh until he caught her paw in his palm. Looking directly into the human's eyes, Pearly reached further to rest her paw and foreleg comfortably and calmly on his forearm.

Dowg had paid special attention to Pearly's displays, and I convinced him to help Will by offering him a place to stay near Boulder. This may sound strange for a few reasons— not the least of which is that Dowg is effectively homeless and resides most of the year in Boulder's Central Park. He sleeps in a very large but movable plastic tub procured from the sympathetic owner of McGuckins Hardware after his previous tub was destroyed by football hooligans. Douglas Snopes, a former banker known to nearly everyone as Dowg, now spends most of his time with a pack of dogs, begging and bantering on the Pearl Street Mall and CU campus.

Will downed the shot of tequila, chased it with a tug of beer and grimaced as the liquid fire made its way to his gut. After shaking off the shiver it sent through his body, Will felt the warmth of the shot enter his bloodstream and relax his tattered nerves. They sat quietly for a moment, and Will pondered the offer of a room. Aside from his truck, what else did he have to lose?

"I hope you like to work out," Dowg winked, slowly lifting his heavy beer with an exaggerated bicep curl and twisted grin.

Chapter 2 - The Swift Dog Gym

You would be correct to assume that I myself enjoy a good workout. However, the depth, intensity, and frequency of my workouts depends entirely on others, including you. So you know, I don't consider my battles with your ridiculous emotions to be workouts—that's just work—a job, an obligation. My funland, similar to your kind's recreation, is questionland. You could think of it like a park or playground for me to frolic in. I have had some good workouts with the humans, especially that CU Boulder bunch, including our emotionally bruised and banged up Will Fiedler.

Will accepted the offer for a "room" at Dowg's friend Houndman's place, with the understanding of Dowg's definition of working out. As you can see there, nearly in the center of the picture, sprawled out on the steps reading, Dowg is no stranger to physical activity, or for that matter, the physical hardships of homelessness. He is as lean and well-muscled as any twenty-something in the mighty Republic of dog-loving hikers, bikers, triathletes, climbers and Olympians. Dowg simply lacks the pretentiousness of the Boulderites, despite lauding their appreciation for healthy food and exercise.

I just as well point out here that Samuel and Houndman are mostly responsible for instilling in Dowg a zest for strength, endurance and hardihood. In the photo, Samuel is the one in the green, left of center, in discussion with several individuals including the *Swift Dog Gym* owner and operator, Houndman. He's there in the red, arms folded, watching and listening to Samuel.

It is important to understand that the mysterious picture has actually been manipulated and is probably misleading you even as our story begins. To be sure, Houndman is no diminutive beardless figure. Half Arapaho Indian and half mutt-mix white, he was a star athlete and wrestler in his youth. He joined the Marine Corps and received a Purple Heart for his courageous fighting at the Battle of Tanaga early in the Pipelineistan wars before settling down on the edge of Jamestown.

He learned to live simplistically off the grid—mostly from Samuel—Houndman would walk miles to see and converse with him. This sort of thinking was passed on to Dowg, who lives well off the grid in Boulder's Central Park. In terms of the questions these men have posed and others have pondered for many years, it's been most interesting in my work with your kind over the generations to provide a reasonable answer to the question: *What does it mean to be a man?*

For Will and his new arrangements at the **Swift Dog Gym**, this first meant covering rent. Contrary to how many of you work out indoors with iron and machines, Will was tasked with work in the outdoors using the weight of wood and tools of iron. Houndman, who heated his cabin with wood in the winter, would provide Will with a bed, contingent on his cutting, splitting, and stacking the entirety of next winter's four cords of firewood to dry. Yes, it's true, I convinced Will to accept the offer, and given his most recent trifecta, it didn't take much conversation to arrive at a decision.

The **Swift Dog Gym** was located at the edge of the small community of Jamestown, Colorado approximately 15 minutes outside of the mighty Republic. Situated along James Creek, Houndman's property comprised of his cabin and several smaller structures, including an earthen den that would be Will's quarters for the semester. Along the northern boundary, next to the creek, was the "gym." The floor of the gym was a neat carpet of pine, fir and spruce bark contained in a large but tidy circle. On the edge of the circle was stacked a large mound of timber, mostly softwoods, but including some smaller maple, ash and elm logs.

When Will arrived to survey the required work and living quarters, he was greeted by Houndman's gentle and pure, white hound dog, Cassee. In exactly the same manner as Pearly in the tavern, Cassee greeted Will by sitting back on her haunches and pawing gently but repeatedly for his hand. Obliging her with a smile, Will held her paw and let the hound look directly into his eyes. Finding him satisfactorily trustable and honest, the pure white hound softly licked his hand.

Such behavior by the dogs thus far in our story cannot be overlooked. For those of you who love and appreciate dogs, like Dowg and Houndman, significant weight is put on the reactions of the dog to specific people. Will did not know it at the time, but he had passed the first and most important test: being selected by the dogs.

In my opinion, a decent word for Will's earthen living quarters would be den, although cave, cabin or hut would suffice. He could see that many years ago it had been carefully built into the ground and covered with dirt and rocks. The roof and outer walls were overgrown with grasses and fading summer wildflowers, save for some Indian paintbrushes, which remained bright scarlet. Outside, to the left of the den's front door, was a hand pump for water and some sturdy wood and stone furniture. Behind the den was the outhouse. Through the top of the earthen mound of dirt and rock, a small metal chimney protruded on the north side. On the south side, a small set of solar panels stared steadily at the sun, and the sun glared heatedly back.

Inside, the temperature was cool, and the room was lit only by the light passing through a small glass window in the door. Will used the flashlight feature on his device to survey the floor and walls of earth and stone and the large supporting timbers in the ceiling. Finding the lone lamp in the room, he illuminated a single wooden bed opposite a small wood stove, which faintly emitted the scent of Ponderosa Pine creosote. A sturdy wooden table and chair were set against the west wall next to the door, each made by hand with a chainsaw from beetle-kill pine. The natural beauty of the rugged furniture neatly matched the supporting timbers of the ceiling and three walls of the den.

Over time, the notably blue-grey and purple features of the flesh of beetle kill pine furniture had aged to blend perfectly with the blue-grey granite in which the den had been built and extended outward. The light of the solitary lamp was too dim to see the entirety of the space, so Will cast the flashlight on his device onto the back of the den. There he saw a spacious lair at the rock's base, easily large enough to comfortably accommodate a dog or a human. Upon closer inspection of the rock wall and smaller den, Will noticed writing chiseled into the stone above it. Some of the inscriptions appeared aged, as if written years ago, while others seemed more recent. Will blew off a thin layer of dust from the rock, focused his light on the various lines, and began with what seemed like the oldest ones.

I would prefer a state of madness than a life of pleasure.

Philosophy is the art of seeing things for what they are.

Reason is the foundation of virtue.

States are doomed when they are unable to distinguish bad men from good men.

The most important learning to occur in life is learning how to get rid of anything to unlearn.

Virtue is a weapon that cannot be taken away.

A wise man is guided in his public acts not by established laws, but by the law of virtue.

The happy life is the only goal and the final aim of philosophy.

The love of money is the mother city of all evils.

I looked into the abyss and the abyss looked back at me.

The greatest enemy of freedom is the state.

Freedom of speech is the most beautiful thing in the world.

Live in accordance with natural laws.

Men of worth are friends.

Women are made to be loved, not understood.

Honor is simply the morality of superior men.

Faith may be defined briefly as an illogical belief in the occurrence of the improbable.

On one issue, at least, men and women agree: they both distrust women.

The most dangerous man to any government is the man who is able to think things out.

A patriot must always be ready to defend his country against his government.

Grown men do not need leaders.

You can't fight City Hall, but you can goddamn sure blow it up.

Just think, right now as you read this, some guy somewhere is getting ready to hang himself.

By and large, language is a tool for concealing the truth.

"Where am I?" Will thought to himself, stirring conversation with me. Yes, I convinced him to re-read the writings in the rock and to be sure not to skip the third quote—it's a personal favorite of mine.

Chapter 3 - Long Wednesday

We would likely agree that language is also a tool for illuminating truth, which happens to be among my specialties for willing listeners. In our story, this occurred most in two different but somewhat similar contexts with many of the same individuals.

To be sure, the picture that I have referenced, and will reference again later, was actually taken at *Weekly Seminar*. You could say that I was a founding member, but *Weekly Seminar* at CU on Fridays was formally organized by Broad for professors and graduate students of Colorado's Front Range universities. You can see them in the picture, and you can see Broad, just left of the middle, in the red, with his index finger pointed skyward.

You may have noted in the picture a writer with disheveled hair, leaning against the pillar on the right in a half-sitting position. That's Ben Blair, an avid climber and mountaineer from Estes Park, Colorado. He mostly keeps to himself, his rocks and his writing. A student of Media, Communication, and Information, Ben was in his second year of his Masters of Fine Arts in Critical Media Studies at CU Boulder. He met Will and Aldo last August at *Weekly*

Seminar, and they became good friends inside and outside of academia.

Have you ever noticed that many outdoor enthusiasts have preferences for their recreation resource? Our graduate students are no different.

Ben's preferences involved rock, especially the vertical stuff. Baby-faced Will by contrast, grew up with preferences involving water, especially swimming, paddling and even rowing at CSU as an undergraduate student. You might be able to tell this from the size of his arms and shoulders. That's Will, there in the bottom right of the picture, in the grey/green, with his right hand on another student's shoulder.

Next to Will is Aldo Pierce, in blue, helping a peer understand the formulas on Dr. Schwede's tablet. Aldo's preferences involve wildlife, whether hunting or fishing, early in the morning or late at night, in the mountains, on the plains or in the oceans. Aldo found his leisure passion for life early on, and I really had little to do with it. Since he was a small boy, he was seldom seen indoors but could be found on the rivers with a dog and a rod, or in the field and woods with rifles and shotguns.

On this particular Wednesday in our story, rock was the resource, and bagging Longs Peak was the goal. Yes, it's true, only about half of those that attempt Rocky Mountain National Park's only 14,000 plus foot peak ever make it to the summit. Each year a number of your kind are killed on Longs Peak, whether by the wind, freezing temperatures, falling or falling rocks. Like big rivers, big mountains command respect, and they will punish anyone, the prepared or unprepared, the skilled or unexperienced, for even the slightest of mistakes in decision-making. Go prepared, and be sure to invite me along, but don't expect a same-day rescue off Longs Peak if you take a fall.

Our three graduate students departed Boulder at 3:30 am and headed towards the Peak to Peak Hwy, heading north on Hwy 7 past Saint Malo's Chapel on the Rock. Ben and I were discussing preparedness for the 14 mile round trip summit, the weather and gear when they turned left towards the trailhead.

Relying mostly on Ben and his mountaineering knowledge and experience, they conducted a gear check near the ranger station.

"Water?" Check.

"Water filter?" Check.

"Food?" Check.

"Rain gear?" Check.

"Extra layer of clothes?" Check.

"Sunscreen, hat & sunglasses?" Check.

"Change of socks?" Check.

"Headlamps?" Check.

"Phones?" Check.

"A sturdy Sherpa with a bag of top-shelf cannabis and a backpack full of beer?"

"He might be running late this morning," Will grinned in reply adjusting his headlamp.

"I have the map and compass," Ben said.

"And I have the ropes," Aldo added.

At mile 1.75, they sat briefly to drink water and watch the horizon light up a new day. Will could hear the soothing trickles and gurgles of the mountain riparian feeding the trailside brooks with cold, clear snowmelt. Staying on the left trail at mile 2.5, the trio ascended towards the tree line, past a small patch of windswept Twisted Krummholz pines. Glimpsing a small figure, Aldo squinted to see a White

Tailed Ptarmigan standing neatly camouflaged against the lichen-covered boulders. Big sky, fewer life forms, massive rock, and cold, thin, windy air greeted them, and the Pikas loudly chirped their warnings.

At mile 3.5, they reached Chasm Junction where they approached the solar-powered dehydrating toilet built there.

"That's a nifty looking shitter."

"Do you think that engineer knows his shit?"

By the time they approached the Boulder Field at mile six for lunch, the elevation was 12,800 feet and Will was bringing up the rear, pausing occasionally as his lungs and body worked harder for each heavy step. He could feel a slight headache coming on, and his stomach began to feel indifferent to taking food and water. As the Boulder Field and bivvy sites came into view, invisible forces propelling powerful winds swept down and around from the massive mountain peak composed of more intimidating rock than Will had originally expected.

Finding some protection from the wind among the boulders, the trio lunched on mostly nuts, jerky, fresh and dried fruits, and cheese, taking in with satisfaction the panoramic view. Yes, it's true, I helped a Yellow Bellied

Marmot make off with Will's entire Ziploc bag of GORP. He lunged half-heartedly for the thief's loot, nearly falling off his boulder seat, but he was no match for the marmot's speed.

Scanning the many large rocks of the Boulder Field to the top of the towering north face of Longs Peak, Ben paused and stared at the visible top of the Diamond. Will looked on and took a deep breath to settle his nauseous stomach and soothe his headache. It was colder, so they opened their packs for their jackets as the chilly winds whipped them with consistent reminders to respect the peak.

The trail became uneven and occasionally indistinguishable as they ascended toward the bottom of the North Face and the base of the slabs. Their pace slowed as they circumnavigated the boulders; they hopped, scrambled and jumped over and around them, taking deep breaths at each landing on the uneven and sometimes unsteady rock. After falling the second time, Will confirmed to himself again that rock was not his preferred recreation resource, especially as he watched Ben leap along the boulders with great agility and ease. Reaching Chasm View first, Ben looked into the full face of the Diamond, which simply stared back at him without acknowledgment or the slightest change of expression.

Chasm Lake, a thousand feet below, glowed turquoise blue and glittered in the shimmering reflections of the high-altitude sun. They drank and rested, watching the misty fingers of cloud vapor drift across Chasm Lake and smoothly caress the Diamond's long, flat face. Following Ben to the base of the Cable Route on the North Face, they organized their gear for the ascent.

Ropeless and using spider-like movements on sure holds to free-climb the route, Ben began working his way up the short pitch. They watched as he momentarily clung to the rock each time the buffeting gusts of wind made efforts to blow him off the face, aided by the surface area of his backpack acting like a sail. Timing his moves between ever stronger gusts of wind, our sure-limbed climber scaled the 140 feet and disappeared over the ledge.

Will and Aldo looked and listened, waiting for Ben to sling the rope down the pitch for their climb up. Nothing and no one appeared with the exception of a deafening clap of thunder. The hair on their arms tingled with the static electric air, and their bodies shook from the dissipating rumble of the thunder's report. They looked back up to see

Ben hurriedly scurrying back onto the pitch. When the first raindrop hit them, Ben had only descended partially down the rock into the vapor fingers and violent clouds suddenly enveloping the fully exposed peak at 14,000 feet.

The second boom of lightning induced thunderous applause, brought stronger winds, rain and ping-pong ball sized hail together for a thorough pelting of our mountaineering students. Everything around them, the air and the rocks, shook and buzzed in submission to the fury. Yes, it's true, I helped Ben off that rain-soaked pitch without a fall. To his credit, he knew when to listen and better yet, when not to listen, when to tune out the buffeting externalities of stormy weather and focus only on my voice and the holds on the route.

This analogy may or may not ring with familiarity, but it certainly does for me. It's true, I have competitors, the most formidable of which are the storm-ridden emotions of your kind. I've witnessed more death, destruction, and despair emanate from your unpredictable emotions, from your minds losing focus on the holds, from not listening to me. Your evolution has seen to it that you are born with my most formidable foe, yet listening to me requires continuous effort and practice for years. It's not fair.

Worse, my bitter enemy has been endowed with astonishing strength and power over you. But such are the artifacts of the evolution of your species.

You would be partially correct in concluding that this grand competition would be job security for me. Or that I'm a good sport and exhibit a positive attitude when you allow my stormy enemy to squelch my voice. The reality is that in my line of work, the best job security is when I can operate under the circumstance of you having beaten our enemy, your emotions, yourself.

My strong preference is that you simply kill them, and kill them all, as soon as possible. I realize that this approach may seem oversimplified and harsh, but the stakes are far too high if we let them live, worsened dramatically if we let them rule. Some say they can't be even killed; I say that they can. This does not imply that we quit trying; it merely signifies that we must rough them up regularly, beat them down daily, and whenever we can, throw a death blow. From centuries of experience, I can tell you that it will not likely end in a final battle to win the lifelong war. If there is victory, it will be achieved by winning one skirmish at a time, over time.

Not that our trio trapped at 14,000 feet were feeling victorious, but they did feel the sting of fat, icy raindrops pelting them from every direction. The rocks trembled and the air buzzed with every hot white electrified flash followed by its thunderous report. Still fully exposed to fall potential and lightning, they scurried and scrambled with bodies low, using their arms and hands when necessary, to the low indentions below and beside the nearest boulders. Under these sort of near-zero visibility conditions, there are really only a few options, and Ben chose the best one in my opinion—wait it out.

They were pelted by the stinging rain, wind and thunderous lightning claps for just under an hour. A cold but light rain rode the winds at every angle when they emerged from the boulders, drenched and shivering with cold. Ben, the worst of them—he had no time to put on raingear—we were busy focusing on the holds and descending. Looking over the many wet, dark and slick rocks of the Boulder Field, they began the seven mile hike out. The rumble of thunder behind Long's westward face followed them with its clear warning of more weather approaching.

"Move fast, but move smart," I told Ben, who echoed the same to his companions.

They only took three falls in total crossing the Boulder Field, and Will was the owner of them all. But with nothing broken and no serious bleeding, he picked himself back up and limped along in his soaking wet socks and boots. Six miles to go.

Will could just see Ben and Aldo ahead on the trail, enveloped in a misty fog that was settling over the tundra above tree line. I convinced him that changing his socks might prevent more blisters similar to the ones developing on his toes and sole. He was able to lengthen his limp, catch up, and briefly enjoy the comforts of damp socks and waterlogged feet inside wet boots.

It was just past four miles to go when a second, but smaller, thunderstorm sufficiently re-soaked them and their footwear. But this didn't dampen their increasingly jovial spirits with each blister- inducing step closer to the trailhead and their vehicle. Cold and hungry, they marched on with thoughts of the warm food and cold beers awaiting them in Glen Haven, not far away.

"Why does Anthony call these suppers *Wednesday Night Services*?" Ben asked.

Chapter 4 - WNS August

Wednesday Night Services is actually a spoof expression. But you would have to know more about our hospitable host at the Glen Haven Inn, Anthony Cornell, to make sense of it. You can see him there in the picture in the bottom left corner, in blue, perusing a recently published book of recipes. But don't be fooled by his image or let it mislead you about the Truth. In this case, no one has ever seen Anthony put on weight, shave his beard, or wear vines around his head, yet that is how he was portrayed. For lack of a better word, I would describe him as alternative, but not any more or less than any other characters captured in the picture.

To put it plainly, as is my preference, Anthony's WNS is mostly a spoof on Christianity, but it includes any group that is gawd-fearing and praying. Given the traditions of many faith-based institutions to meet for prayer services on Wednesday evenings, Anthony chose the same evening for his suppers. However, it was not open to the public, only to the academics and students who attended *Weekly Seminar* at CU.

Yes, it's true, I convinced Anthony that living a life of fear is pointless, that having fear of a gawd or gawds is silly, and that praying to them is much sillier. For him, the absurdity is exacerbated when people grovel and beg to their gawds in prayer primarily for evil against one another. To counter, Anthony put on delightful and healthy spreads of food, beverage, and the conditions for varied and sensible conversations among attendees.

Glen Haven, Colorado is located at the confluences of West Creek, Fox Creek, and the North Fork of the Big Thompson River along Larimer County Road 43 near Estes Park. Operated by Anthony and his staff, The Glen Haven Inn B & B also provided fine dining in the evenings by reservation for renowned garden to table cuisine. For WNS, there was more of the same and then some, usually on the large wooden deck that jutted westward from the inn, overlooking the gardens and West Creek. Combining fresh mountain air, music, and conversation, the ambiance has always been inviting to me, and never have I missed a WNS.

Key players in attendance do include Houndman, Dowg and their canine companions. Since Anthony is a vegetarian, Houndman arrives early to enjoy Odell's IPA and to smoke meats in his electric smoker for the omnivores and carnivores in attendance. Dowg's self-imposed duties were to hike the dogs along the trails of the Glen Haven area, some public, but he stuck mostly to lesser-travelled trails made by the locals. Seeing dogs hunt, play, and run about off-leash at their liberty in the woods always brought him a profound sense of contentment and rekindled his deep-seated love for anarchy.

Metro, another WNS regular, usually arrived before supper with his guitar and gear to provide the live music for WNS attendees. You can see him there in the picture closest to Dowg; his back is to the photographer. As you can likely tell from the picture, Dowg is mostly indifferent to Metro, a master's student in Music Education at CU. Dowg and I have discussed artist types, or really anyone that he has determined is a Peter Pan variety among your kind's males, and he thought that Metro fit the criteria. But it was actually Halsey who gave him the name Metro, and Dowg has never stopped piling on. Halsey is in the top left of the picture, standing next to Houndman and looking at Samuel. A tall, muscular, military man, Halsey was very good friends with Samuel. Both were actually veterans of the same foreign wars.

Central to *Weekly Seminar,* and thus the picture, are Professors Broad and Spencer, who also attend WNS.

Broad is professor and chair of the Department of Philosophy at CU, a prolific writer, on the Board of CU Regents, the originator of *Weekly Seminar*, and a frequent faculty sponsor for interdisciplinary talks and conferences. You might actually recognize his likeness; he's in the center of the picture with his finger pointed upward. Like Houndman and Anthony, his image has been manipulated and may mislead you about Broad because of his startling resemblance to Leonardo da Vinci. However, the photographer did correctly capture his build and fondness for abstract concepts.

Before embarking on a long career in higher education, the young Ambrose Stotlar had planned to become an Olympic wrestler. After having been decisively pinned at the US National Championship Team Trials, thus ending his Olympic dreams, he decided to pursue education. Ambrose even changed his name to better reflect his past as a wrestler and his opinion of the size of his back and shoulders and has been known as Broad ever since. It should be noted, and Broad would agree, that Samuel was his favorite professor. Even I would agree that Samuel is a master professor, and in terms of conversing with me, he is a master listener. Not many of your kind have brains wired like that solid superstar, Sam.

Next to Broad in the center of the picture is the younger Dr. Spencer. In his left hand he is holding one of his books; with his right, he is suggesting the importance of the concrete details of the matter being discussed. I can attest to Spencer's unusually rare talents and abilities. He also possesses an incredibly powerful and versatile mind for a human, is a master listener, and has applied our conversations to many different topics.

Yes, it's true, some years ago the young Spencer was actually Broad's best doctoral student at CU. But over the course of their work, Spencer and Broad eventually diverged in their philosophies of science, research, and even world perspectives to such a degree that Spencer left Broad and Boulder behind. He was quickly hired by Colorado State University, and in short time became Director of the College of Veterinary Medicine and Biomedical Sciences at CSU in Fort Collins, Colorado. The son of a physician himself, Spencer has become the preeminent biomedical scientist in the US and is among the most published authors in multiple disciplines in the world.

Our three soggy-booted, weather-battered graduate students headed down the switchbacks from Estes Park to Glen

Haven into the warmth of the August sunshine at 8,000 feet to join the others at WNS. Will limped up the stairs behind Aldo and Ben to the sounds of laughter, clinking silverware and glass mingled with the soft hum of conversations. Metro was sitting on a small stool strumming his guitar and singing a song no one seemed to recognize. Overlaying these sounds were the gentle wisps of alder smoke, which floated randomly from the metal edges of Houndman's salmon-filled smoker. Next to it was a large cooler of beer and beyond it, husked corn, and sweet peppers and onions were roasting on the grill.

Will was the last of the students to arrive at the cooler where he overheard a very tall, rather diplomatic-looking man ask Anthony about a lecture he had given. Anthony was working the grill, and he put on another round of soaked corn before answering the tall, well-dressed man with neatly-trimmed white eyebrows that rested atop his flat, expressionless bearded face.

"I most certainly stirred debate with my questions, especially among the more hardline Christian types. I posed the trilemma in this way: Why does gawd allow evil to exist? If he is willing to eliminate it, but can't, then is he impotent? If he is able, but unwilling, is he malevolent? If he is neither willing nor able, is he a malevolent impotent? If he is both willing and able, why does evil exist?"

Will pondered these rapid-fire questions from the renowned chef before taking a swig of his 90 Schilling and inching closer to the grill.

"Zeno, it's always seemed strange to me that such tremendous fear of gawd would be allowed to keep a person from being free and realizing all that the world has to offer through our senses; the only way to experience anything at all really," Anthony said. "There are no gawds that have influence over our lives, so why live in fear of punishment when we could be seeking and enjoying a life full of tranquility, free of mental and physical pain?" He opened the grill top and rotated the corn and sweet peppers.

"In your belief system, is pleasure the chief aim in life?" Zeno asked, his face still, his gaze steady like the face of the Diamond on Longs. You can see him there in the bottom leftmost corner of the picture, in a blue hood, next to the baby and Anthony.

"I know where you're headed with this Zeno," Anthony replied with a smile and shake of his head. "No need to blame me for undermining traditional morality systems, faith-based or otherwise. Seems clear to me that if we could eliminate the fear of gawd and death, people would be able to reach true happiness from the pleasure of their senses in this gawdless mechanistic world of atoms. Enjoy some good food, enjoy some good friends, keep your body and mind healthy and know that death and gawd mean nothing to us."

Zeno nodded his head once slightly and slowly asked, "Does this search for pleasure contain any calls for restraint, or can I aim for the logical extremes of your propositions?"

"I don't recommend it, but you could try to indulge yourself in whatever you please," Anthony responded smiling. "If, say, eating too many high-fat, white-breaded cheeseburgers or consuming too much high-fructose corn syrup leads to stomach pain and indigestion, I would recommend foods that are more satisfying and healthy, ones that provide tranquility for the mind and ease in bodily digestion."

Anthony threw open the grill, removed the corn and vegetables and placed them on a table next to the rice pilaf and couscous salad. Taking up the most space on the table was a large colander of freshly picked kale, chard, arugula, spinach, and lettuces topped with pansy and nasturtium flowers. Broad and Spencer were the last to make themselves plates; both had remained seated with their beverages, locked in a discussion while the others lined up to load their plates.

"What's that smell?" Houndman said, raising his nose to the air as if to assess a scent coming from the general direction of Broad and Spencer.

"Don't inhale," Dowg said. "Or step in it," he quipped, rolling his eyes and smirking.

"Your propositions on how men should be governed are untenable and would bring ruin to any collective order," Broad said in his perpetually soft, weak voice, "Freedom is found in unity of purpose and devotion to the larger political community."

"Submitting to the collective order disallows support for the individual citizen to reach his full potential," Spencer quickly responded in his slightly lisping voice. "I hold that people can only be free if they are individuals who can live a self-determined life of liberty. In this case, liberty also implies freedom from government interference in our lives."

"Sounds like naturally occurring anarchy to me," Dowg interjected. "Liberty—raw, unfiltered, and unencumbered by the institutions of government and society."

"We might all agree that the goal of politics is to make for a good, virtuous people," Broad countered. "Which is why in my system, a good citizen might work in the morning, fish in the afternoon and write poetry in the evening. In your system Spencer, expect them to sleep all morning, play video games all afternoon, maybe shop, and then watch movies all evening.

"What is more," Broad went on, "have them governed by equally ignorant politicians and demagogues. This is what democracy brings." He finally took a bite of smoked salmon, followed by a sip of wine.

Before Spencer could reply, Dowg interjected. "Sounds like another great reason to go with anarchy! Lying politicians or lying tyrants of the oligarchy, pick your poison, professors; both systems are easily corruptible, and both are doomed over the span of a few generations. What else could make it any more obvious than mound after mound of demonstrable lies from our *supposed leaders* in the *supposed news*?" Dowg queried.

"Are you all talking about politics again?" Anthony inquired, frowning in obvious disapproval. "Have some rhubarb cobbler, maybe a little more wine and beer, jump in the hot tub if you need to relax from all that political talk."

Will took advantage of all three options and was joined by his peers. They were recalling the day's recreation experiences when Halsey strolled over and spun the top off a beautifully engraved flask nearly full of Michter's 20-year-old Single Barrel Bourbon.

"This ought to cure what ails you," Halsey said with a smirk, handing the flask to Will to take a tug and to pass around.

"So Samuel tells me that you're helping Houndman out for the semester," Halsey grinned. "Have you gone hunting with Dowg yet?" he asked mischievously, turning to look towards Dowg and Pearly. Sensing that she might be a part of the conversation, Pearly wagged her tail and trotted over, followed by Dowg.

Will didn't know how to answer the question or even what it meant or could mean. Judging from Halsey's wolfish grin, and feeling the warmth of the hot tub and bourbon, he thought it best to play along.

"Hunting for what?"

"Mostly rodents," Halsey replied quickly in what appeared to be a code that kindled the vibrant twinkle in Dowg's eyes and resulted in a wide grin of his own. "They've been known to chase bigger game," Halsey said to the students, "but like any other worthwhile endeavor among men, *Hunt Club* membership comes with initiation and testing. Isn't that about right Dowg?"

"That's right," Dowg chimed in, "not everyone can keep up with me."

"What are a few initiations you've had people do for *Hunt Club*?" Aldo asked. Since he was a hunter, he thought that it might involve long hikes, marksmanship, and campfires surrounded by Hooters babes serving them beer.

"To run with me and mine," Dowg said choosing his words rather carefully, "you have to be in shape mentally and physically, and this only comes from training. I conduct the training and instill a sense of *action-oriented shamelessness* in all members."

"*Action-oriented shamelessness?*"

"Yes. For example, I once had a philosophy major carry a large dead and rotting carp up and down Pearl Street. He was to ask the most well-dressed shoppers if they would like a sample taste of it," Dowg explained in thoughtful recollection. "His disdain for consumerism I found delightful, and his courage truly refreshing."

"Another student I had balance a large piece of cheese on his head before entering the CU administrative building. Finding our way to the offices of the Provost and President, he asked anyone there if they would like some cheese to go with their decision to fire a beloved professor unafraid to speak and write his mind," Dowg recalled.

"A good prank, with or without words, on deserving individuals or organizations will do," Dowg explained more specifically. "Some have heckled politicians, preachers, professors, lawyers, CEOs and shoppers of all economic strata. Anyone fooled by, or in collusion with the large and dishonest institutions of society are the prey of our hunting fields. The test is that you can't show any shame or fear; if you are embarrassed, you can't become a member—that's the initiation," Dowg explained. "The reality is that once you've unmasked dishonesty in yourself," Dowg rubbed Pearly's neck, "and you have no regard for what other people think of you, then we can go hunting to unmask dishonesty in others—bag a few weasels, maybe a trophy buck, sheep for sure." He turned his head to see Metro walking over to them.

Metro arrived, towel in one hand, raspberry wheat beer in the other, and his man-bun up.

"Mind if I join?"

"You have to take shot of bourbon; it's pool rules," Halsey needled, spinning the top off the flask for him.

"No thanks, I can't drink liquor straight," he replied.

"You could try washing it down with your wine cooler," Dowg chided, unenthused about including Metro in the discussion.

"We were just talking about fucking shit up," Halsey said gauging his reaction. "Do you have a cause Metro?"

"A cause?" Metro paused to think. "Well, I wrote a letter, made a sign and marched in a rally for social justice at CU this year. We won funding for new restrooms, so any member of the LGBTQ community would feel comfortable, safe, secure, and free from hate on our campus." Metro beamed with the pride most paired with virtue signaling.

"How about you Aldo?" Halsey quickly asked, seeing Dowg roll his eyes at Metro.

Not every cause is the same, as you will find in the mighty Republic, but having one at all is typically the mark of someone I have conversed with. For example, I once convinced a math mind to take up the cause of converting the entire world to the Metric system. No more pounds, miles, feet, yards or tons of American exceptionalism, only metric uniformity and efficiency in weights and measures. Your cause is likely different; maybe it's the poor, battered women, wounded veterans, the environment or your church and family. Maybe your cause is football, a river, UFOs, collecting dolls or just your technological device.

For Aldo, it was the oil and gas industry in Colorado, and its effects on his family's farm outside of Windsor. Contaminated well-water and toxic air particulates from nearby Anadarko Petroleum hydraulic fracturing well sites had all but ended their family ranching business. Aldo's father sued Anadarko, but Mr. Pierce was soon counter-sued for defamation by the fracking company. Unable to sell the farm, and having drained the family's wealth in the lawsuits, the most his dad could do was turn on the kitchen faucet, light it, and burn off the methane.

"Fracking assholes," Aldo muttered taking a swig of Dales Pale Ale. Setting the beer down, he reached into his back pocket and produced a can of dipping tobacco, which he thumped soundly with his forefinger to pack for a pinch.

Ben divulged that his older brother, a professional athlete turned Army Special Forces Ranger, had been killed in Afghanistan. His family and I firmly believe that the official explanation for his death was covered up by the Pentagon and press corps. "Or as I like to call them, the presstitutes," Ben said. "Pat was triple-tapped to the forehead at near point blank range, so we know there's more to the explanation, but they won't tell my parents how this could have happened."

Listening to his peers, Will had been enjoying the hot tub's work on his banged up body in combination with the work of the bourbon and beers. He filled Halsey in on his trifecta of big cats, land lords, and mortgage banksters. Halsey and Dowg couldn't contain their laughter when Will told of his father bulldozing their house into the swimming pool to rile Wells Fargo.

Yes, *action* matters. I convinced our three graduate students to commit to an initiation; never mind the ambiguities of Dowg's so-called *Hunt Club*, there is sure to be adventure.

In fairness, peer pressure deserves some credit and our mercenary friend Halsey provided the most:

"Are we going to fuck some shit up or not boys?"

Chapter 5 - The Death of Paul Guarneri

You've likely induced or deduced that I've been helping your kind fuck shit up ever since you quit your nomadic lifestyles of hunting and gathering. Ever since you fell— against your wishes or not—into the nation-state lifestyle of cubicles, cages and factories in large, reeking, lonely and overpopulated cities.

I've had many conversations with your kind about either succumbing to it, adapting to it, or fleeing it, and in fewer cases, even changing it. Dr. Paul Guarneri decided long ago to flee it. You can see him there, bottom left corner, kneeling in the white, reading a book. Not one to fuck shit up in the least, but like the few of your kind that decided to think freely and live independently in privacy, Guarneri made enemies. In my opinion, he didn't deserve to be shot, but I'll let you be the judge.

≡Westword

Ten Members of Secretive Cult Killed Outside Boulder in Firefight with Federal Authorities

Federal law-enforcement officials confirmed the deaths of 10 members of the secret religious cult known as *The*

Dyadic Order of Ratio. The founder and leader of the order, Dr. Paul Guarneri, was also killed in events surrounding the ensuing inferno of their compound near Niwot, Colorado. Officials have not determined the cause of the blaze nor have they been able to determine the identity of three of the victims from remains recovered at the scene.

A witness who called 911 indicated that a dispute occurred at the front gate of the compound with an armed man in paramilitary wear making loud demands to enter the premises and see Guarneri. Turned away by commune security, the armed man left momentarily only to return in a truck. Witnesses explained that he drove his truck at high speed through the gates and crashed the vehicle into the side of the primary commune structure and home of Dr. Guarneri. Witnesses also reported hearing sporadic gunfire and seeing smoke rise from the compound area before the Boulder County Sherriff deputies arrived. It is still unclear to authorities how the fire began.

In a statement from the Federal Bureau of Investigation, officials acknowledged that the compound was under surveillance as part of the nationwide manhunt for two cult members accused of leading an armed coup of the U.S. government last year. In all, 22 people were killed in the bloody Washington DC massacre, and law enforcement officials at the local, state, and federal levels are continuing investigative work for their capture. Officials have been unable to confirm that the fugitives, known only as Damon and Melissa, were among the deceased found at the burned compound.

The Boulder County Medical Examiner issued a statement indicating that three of the victims have been identified as members of the *Dyadic Order of Ratio* and the famed Boulder jam band *Tetractys*. The medical examiner confirmed that Guarneri's cause of death was from a single gunshot wound. Officials have been unable to confirm whether or not any other of the 10 victims were shot before perishing in the compound blaze. In yesterday's press briefing, the Boulder County Sheriff confirmed that Guarneri had been shot through the back and that he was found approximately 284 meters away, adjacent to the compound structures. The sheriff also confirmed that Guarneri had been running to escape the blaze and his body was found lying face down on the edge of a bean field bordering the southern perimeter of the commune.

Law enforcement officers are still searching for the armed man believed to have fired the shots and set fire to the compound. The medical examiner's office statement indicated that Guarneri died from a wound consistent with a large caliber rifle and not a handgun. The FBI and the Boulder County Sheriff Department are investigating if agents or deputies fired shots and their justifications for the use of deadly force. Initial ballistics reports indicate that the shot may not have come from the area of the compound's burning structures. One witness described hearing shots from the north and indicated there were multiple shooters.

While it remains unclear who shot and killed Dr. Guarneri, law enforcement officials are continuing their search for his two cult followers accused of high crimes against the US government in a failed coup attempt. The *Dyadic Order of Ratio* has been described as a secret society begun by Guarneri or "The Divine" as he is called among his followers. Authorities have learned that over the past four months Guarneri would not be seen by anyone, would not be interviewed by the media and would only give speeches to his followers from behind a curtain. Investigators believe these behaviors may have influenced the gunman to ram the gates and the primary structure of the commune.

Disciples of the *Dyadic Order of Ratio* dress in white and must adhere to a strict regimen of vegetarianism, music practice, silence and prayer to the number 10. Members abstain from eating beans and from having sex, but if sex must be had, it can only occur in the winter, according to Guarneri's teachings. Several order members were contacted by *Westword* but did not reply to our requests for interviews.

Westword's research on Guarneri reveals that he is no stranger to scandal. Nearly 25 years ago he was acquitted in the trial of the death of CU mathematics professor, Dr. Chip Parsons. Reports indicated that Professors Guarneri and Parsons were co-teaching mathematics during a Semester at Sea and came to an open and heated disagreement about ratio-related computations.

Reports indicate that on the same evening, Parsons fell overboard and drowned. Conflicting accounts of the events were documented, and it remains unclear to this day what occurred. Two witnesses on the cruise ship claimed that Guarneri pushed Parsons overboard after a brief struggle. Dr. Guarneri maintained in his defense that he tried to catch Parsons as he fell, having been sickened by rough seas and an evening meal of beans.

Please contact the FBI field office in Denver or submit a tip electronically if you have any information about fugitives

Damon and Melissa or the criminal activity involving *The Dyadic Order of Ratio* compound fire and shootings.

Chapter 6 - It's Working Out

"Up and at 'em boy!" Dowg barked, rapping his knuckles on the door to Will's earthen cave in Jamestown. "Time to work out!"

Will's device showed 5:30 am.

"Are you sure it wasn't supposed to be at 5:30 *pm?*" Will replied groggily through the unopened door.

Receiving no answer, he slipped on his shorts and Chacos and stepped out of the den into the dawn, rubbing the sleep from his eyes. Looking towards the river, he blinked twice to assure that he was seeing Dowg, butt naked, walking into James Creek. Near him, Pearly waded and sniffed the creek's edge.

"Isn't that water cold?" Will asked, approaching hesitantly.

"It is," Dowg replied before sitting in a deep pool up to his shoulders, "that's the whole point; it's uncomfortable. Mmmmmrrrrrrrrr," Dowg growled as he fought back his body shivering in the cold creek water.

"Well, what are you waiting for?" Dowg asked. "Let's see how long we can go before getting out," he suggested with a shivering smile. "Rrrrrrrrrrrrrrrgh," he growled, "this feels great!"

Will eased into the water, began to shiver and was soon overcome with the intense need to urinate.

"And no pissing in the creek," Dowg said before he submerged his entire head and torso into the water of the deep pool.

In short time, Will's teeth began to chatter as the shivers made their way up his body and through his neck. He worked his arms and hands in a swimming fish motion to warm himself while the creek's current took his warmth downstream like a quiet and efficient thief.

Dowg re-appeared on the surface of the deep pool, floating on his back with his feet pressing on the stones.

"Doesn't that feel good boy?" Dowg said facing the sky before sitting back into the creek pool.

Will fought off a bout of shuddering and shaking, his teeth chattering and his stomach screaming for warm calories. "Damn... good... time..... Dowg!" he managed to say.

Like Will, you might be wondering why Dowg, a homeless man, would want to make himself and Will feel so uncomfortable with the pain and suffering associated with hypothermia. It is likely that you, like many of the residents of Boulder that have ever interacted with Dowg, think that he has gone mad and lost his mind. Yes, it's true. I convinced him some years ago that the best workout for the humans is to embrace hardships. Since Dowg has taken this type of sport to a new level, he may appear to be mad, but he sees himself as an Olympian. In fairness, Houndman, and even Samuel deserve most of the credit. In terms of listening to me, Dowg has applied a logic to living that is considered by most of your species to be extreme.

Given my specialty in reaching logical conclusions, I first convinced Dowg that human happiness springs from living a virtuous life. He is not the first of your kind to converse with me on this matter. With few exceptions, the individuals in the picture believed the same about achieving happiness. But what differentiates Dowg from many others is that I convinced him that virtue can be taught and learned since you're not born with it.

"As we know, there are really only two kinds of training that matter: mental and bodily training, and each is incomplete without the other," Dowg said walking with Will through the cool morning air to Houndman's cabin for breakfast, both still shivering. "Nothing in life has any chance of succeeding without strenuous practice, for the growth mindset is capable of overcoming anything."

They were met by Houndman's old white dog, Cassee, and the smell of bacon frying on the side burner of the grill on the back deck. Cassee greeted Will by sitting back on her haunches and extending a paw for a shake. Will was now familiar with the secret shake protocol and shook hand to paw, smiling at the white dog. As was customary at Houndman's, upon finishing breakfast, they put their plates on the floor for the dogs to slick clean of egg yolk and bacon grease. Some might find this practice repulsive if not unsanitary, but for Houndman, it was the efficient conservation of resources.

"Why work out with iron bars and discs on hamster-wheels inside some smelly gym when you could be working out with wood in the most sacred gym of all—the outdoors?" Houndman asked before taking in a deep breath of the cool, clean Rocky Mountain morning air at the *Swift Dog Gym*.

They entered Houndman's workshop where Will inhaled the faint smell of gasoline and oil mixed with the fresh scent of evergreens that permeated the small, tin-roofed structure. Inside, Will could see that the contents of the shop were almost entirely hard, cold metal tools. On the far wall hung several beautifully handcrafted bucksaws and other smaller bowsaws. The entire south-facing wall of the shop was covered in hanging crosscut saws of various sizes, old and new, including two-man felling and bucking crosscut saws with their many long teeth of sharpened steel.

Opposite the south wall, a sturdy wooden work bench ran the length of the shop. On it sat a large vice and tools, and below it were chainsaws, chains, bars, and parts. These were overseen by wrenches, screwdrivers and woodworking tools, all hanging in their designated places on the wall. In the corners of the shop were splitting mauls, mauls, wedges, a few hatchets and numerous axes with wooden and graphite handles.

"These are our weapons," Houndman proclaimed. "And it's really how I see virtue to be. A weapon. And one that cannot be taken away from you," he said reaching for a large chainsaw beneath the bench. "And one that must be sharp," he added selecting a round metal file from the tools. Houndman showed Will how to sharpen the teeth of the saw, maintain the fluids, and other dos and don'ts of using such a powerful weapon.

"And like developing virtue, you'll need to put some ass into it!" Houndman yelled over the roar of the chainsaw pulled to life. "It's heavy lifting!" he shouted before burying the sharp teeth of the roaring metallic tool into a large, knot-covered Ponderosa Pine log. Will watched the screaming saw spray strips of pine meat and sawdust in a neat and steady stream to the ground. The sharp, gnashing teeth of the howling tool, invisible to the naked eye, cut through the log like a sharp Truth through ignorance. After demonstrating the desired length of a firewood round by cutting one himself, Houndman showed Will how to best and safely cut such large logs with such a big, merciless tool.

"Keep your footing and watch what you're doing Will; that weapon takes no prisoners."

Chapter 7 - Jack Hammer

When Will was not cutting wood for his earthen den rent, he was usually on CU's campus, working with weapons of a different nature. In his spacious but cluttered office, Dr. Schwede and Will discussed Will's graduate assistantship research as a component of a Pentagon-funded weapons design project. Specifically, how to hijack and then control air or space craft using remotely-controlled technologies. Dr. Schwede had already developed technologies to accomplish the same in land vehicles and ships at sea, so it was Will's project to develop code to do the same in aerospace. You can see Schwede there in the picture, bottom right, bent over and explaining the solution to a problem on a large tablet on the floor.

"I forgot it!" Schwede suddenly exclaimed, looking at his device to see the meeting reminder that had softly pinged its message of a pre-arranged commitment. Dr. Schwede had previously accepted an invitation from Dr. Roberta Lichter to guest speak at the University of Northern Colorado on the topic of *Advances in Commercial Space Travel for Civilians*. The well-intentioned but easily overcommitted Dr. Schwede could not attend and asked Will to go in his stead. You can see Roberta there in the picture. Dressed in UNC blue and gold, she's standing to Broad's right, just behind Samuel, scowling at Dr. Spencer.

Roberta Lichter is a brassy blonde with a penchant for pantsuits, golden retrievers, positions of power, and the occasional grad student. Fond of wearing the school colors, flashy lapel pins and fake smiles, Dr. Lichter never passed an opportunity to be seen or to scramble up rungs of the administrative ladder. This has indeed strained our relationship; I genuinely cannot tolerate such touchy-feely, silly, selfish emotions for more power and personal recognition. From Assistant Professor to Associate Professor and tenure, to Professor, to Department Chair, to Director of the School of Human Sciences, to Assistant Dean of the College of Natural and Health Sciences, to Dean, to Provost over the entire pile of PhDs. Most expert at self-promotion, nepotism and cronyism, her intended trajectory towards the position of university president was as clear as her disdain for Dowg and Houndman.

Dr. Schwede had sufficient faith in Will to speak a few words and conduct the Q & A at UNC, so he immediately went back to work on his device, and Will made his way to Central Park. Having committed to work out with Dowg for rent-related reasons, Will sought to tell him the change in plans. He came upon Dowg lounging in the warmth of the morning sun, leaning against his large plastic tub, conversing with a Jack Russell Terrier.

Dowg gently rubbed the terrier's neck and ears in his search for owner or veterinarian contact information on the collar. But there was only one tag, and it contained on one side, one word: **Jack**.

Dowg laughed, his eyes bright, as Jack looked at him with the same zest for living. His little nubby tail wagged with friendliness and a sense of adventure even when Dowg made humor of the unoriginality of his name.

"And who might you belong to?" Dowg asked Jack, making his little nub slow to a pace nearing stillness. Jack sat down, put his ears back, and looked Dowg intelligently in the eyes, his own eyes appearing larger and brighter on his seemingly destitute little face.

Yes, it's true. I told Jack that if he wanted out, he should take advantage afforded by the irresistible display of his neotenous Jack Russell features to overcome Dowg. And yes, I told Dowg that a dog like Jack is of more value than the average of your kind, and that any dog lover would take action.

"You like hunting Jack?" Dowg asked with a cheery tone of adventure looking into the dog's bright brown eyes.

Jack stood up, cocked his head sideways and wagged his nub at high frequency. Looking Dowg in the eye, and trying to gauge exactly his tone, Jack cocked his head to the other side to hear or see confirmation of said adventure.

Both consulted me and upon conclusion of our short conversation, we decided to simply take the Jack Russell with us.

"Greeley?" Dowg asked, "Where the aroma of the mounds of sun-cooked stockyard cow shit passes for the smell of money?"

"Great from the ground up?"

"Or is that all ground up?"

"Might be all fracked up."

"Well then, let's go hunting in Greality!" Dowg exclaimed loudly, "I do plenty at CU, some at CSU, and in fairness, we must include UNC!"

They climbed into Will's truck where Jack wagged his nub in full and obvious agreement, straining to see over the dashboard into the wide-open world beyond the windshield.

"Hugs and kisses to Robbie for me!" Dowg shouted, puckering up his lips and making kissing sounds as he watched Will saunter into the south entrance of Gunter Hall at UNC. Dowg strolled about UNC's east campus, and on a large, mowed green lined with trees, he released Jack from the prohibitions of the leash.

Jack zipped full speed towards the nearest squirrel, aiming to cut off any escape routes to trees. Seeing the swift terrier rapidly approaching, the bushy-tailed rodent unenthusiastically scampered up the nearest tree only to stop several feet up the trunk where it scolded Jack from what it thought was a safe distance. Jack neared the base of the tree and slowed only slightly before he half-climbed and half-pushed off the base to gain more altitude for his vertical leap. Reaching the peak of his jump, Jack was nearly nose-to-nose with the now frightened squirrel, which began scrambling up the tree backwards.

Landing neatly on his feet, Jack shot back and forth among the other trees towards the nearest squirrels. His furry little legs morphed into an indiscernible blur at each sprint toward a flicking bushy tail. Several students had gathered near Dowg to watch the brown and white blur with the nubby tail jump, bark and run, until he stopped to squat and shat.

Dowg pulled a small, black plastic bag from his shorts pocket, grabbed Jack's gift, and tied the bag off with a firm knot. Instead of disposing of the bag in the nearest garbage can, he retrieved from the trash a partially torn but still usable manila envelope. Having smashed the bagged gift into the manila envelope, he asked a student passing by for a pen with which he wrote something quickly on the front of the manila envelope.

"Can you tell me where the administration building is located?" Dowg asked, smiling.

Approaching Carter Hall, Dowg pulled from his pocket a headlamp, which he put on before opening the door for our new terrier friend, Jack.

Noting the sign pointing to the president's office on the next floor, Dowg made his way up the stairs to a long corridor laced with administrative offices, cubicles and fake plants. Turning 180 degrees, Dowg began walking backwards down the corridor with his head lamp on a bright blue strobe mode. Jack led the way, headfirst.

"Can I help you sir?" the gentle lady at the front desk of the Provost's office asked, bewildered by the sight of the cute little dog and the grungy, backwards-walking beggar.

"I was about to ask you if there were any honest men around here," Dowg asked while the blue strobes of light bounced off her soft face, "but all I've seen thus far are women." He peered over her shoulder at the all-female office suite.

"Honest men?" the secretary asked, thinking she'd heard him incorrectly.

"Never mind," Dowg said, continuing backwards. A student worker in the office of the graduate school, hunched fixedly over her phone, was so absorbed in texting that she didn't notice either Dowg or Jack walk by, despite the strobe light.

Backing his way into the office of the president, Dowg and Jack were immediately met by another well-dressed, soft-spoken, gentle lady.

"Can I help you sir?" she asked firmly but politely, blinking a little at the light rhythmically hitting her face.

"I've come to meet with the president," Dowg said.

"Do you have an appointment sir?" she asked softly, trying to make sense of the dog, the man and the headlamp all together.

"No mam," Dowg said with equal politeness, "but I have some important information for the president. Would you mind delivering this to her?"

Handing her the manila envelope, Dowg slipped out of the office suite with Jack by his side. The sharply-dressed secretary inspected the manila envelope and found the following written on the front face:

Please find enclosed my nomination for the official symbol and odor of your collusion with the frackers drilling under UNC's campus.

With Love for Clean Air and Frisky Squirrels - Jack

Dowg exited the administration building, cut Jack loose on a large, overfed, and mostly-domesticated squirrel, and pocketed his headlamp. Arriving at Gunter Hall, Jack and Dowg entered a side door to the faculty offices surrounding the main office suite. Here, Dowg paused briefly to read the various research posters on the walls between faculty office doors. Jack was tugging on the leash towards an open office door when they heard the sound of women laughing. Working their way past the posters and around the corner of the office maze, they came upon several women surrounding a grotesquely obese mountain of flesh sitting at a desk. They were giggling at something on her computer screen.

All eyes went to Jack, then to Dowg, and then back to Jack again as he wagged his entire body and stubby nub in the pleasure of meeting new people, especially women to coddle him. As the obese woman shifted to see better, Dowg pitied the chair that squeaked in protest under the massive weight overflowing its stressed and worn arm rests. He could see that her enormous buttocks were stuffed into black stretch pants, and a Denver Broncos jersey struggled to contain the gelatinous contents of her upper half. In front of the mountain, on the desk, was a nameplate, reading *Tricia Lunde—Administrative Assistant.*

Dowg let Jack off the leash to be petted, his little steps slowing as he approached them, his nub wagging with excitement, his brown eyes large and bright.

"Can I help you?" Tricia asked, standing up. Oddly enough, she was barefooted. Her feet were as fat as the rest of her, and her ankles looked uncomfortably swollen.

Perhaps I could be of help to you, Triggly? Dowg thought, silently congratulating the chair for surviving another day of performing its crushing duty.

Tricia paused to look him over, taking in his ragged appearance—the ancient Carhartt pants cut off into shorts, an old pair of retreaded Chacos on his feet, and his torn shirt, mostly unbuttoned to reveal a bony, tanned chest. They stared at each other while Tricia tried to process the beggar and the purpose of his visit.

"Not to worry," Dowg said, "I'm meeting a student here soon."

Bored by the slow conversation, Jack slipped off to explore the various offices and came upon a door left ajar. He pushed the door open enough with his paw to wedge his nose, then body into the office to see that much of it had been decorated with stuffed giraffes collected from the owner's travels abroad. Jack quivered with excitement and his tail pulsed rhythmically as he decided which stuffed animal he would make his own. Like a field-weary soldier or seafaring sailor on leave stepping into a reputable whorehouse, Jack made his selection. He returned to the main office suite proudly carrying a stuffed giraffe, of equal size to himself, in his mouth, by the back of the neck. Jack strutted the stuffed animal about, and then promptly released it, and mounted it, pinching it firmly between his front legs. Confident that his prize was secure, he humped the hapless stuffed animal like a jackhammer in syncopation with every other beat of his wagging nub. A true believer in diversity, Jack humped the stuffed giraffe every which way, from behind, on top, sideways and even the stuffed object's head.

"Hey, stop that!" Tricia shouted, stepping toward Jack to retrieve the freshly-hammered stuffed animal. The giraffe, clearly dominated, had its face pressed hard into the carpet when Jack snatched it up again by the neck and scampered away from Tricia's advance. Darting around a corner of the maze and disappearing momentarily, Jack returned with a different stuffed giraffe, easily twice his size. Again, Jack put the animal down on its side, mounted it, and humped *this* stuffed giraffe sideways, biting its neck and growling in total satisfaction and domination. Jack hammered the defenseless giraffe like a well-tuned athletic machine until he felt the floor trembling as Tricia lumbered towards him.

Jack again grabbed the stuffed giraffe by the neck, juked left, then right, and zipped past Tricia as she whirled her massive frame and attending flesh around to grab at the stuffed animal. Losing her balance, she crashed to the floor with sufficient seismic activity to shake the office walls and rattle the doors. Hearing the commotion, Roberta entered the office suite clearly concerned, but mostly confused, as she took in Tricia rolling around on the floor like a beached whale, Jack humping away at the giraffe, and the ragged beggar bent over with laughter.

Seeing that he was mostly cornered now by the sheer mass of Tricia, the desk, and Roberta, Jack grabbed his oversized hump buddy by the neck and zipped for the corridor with the hope of some privacy in a safe space. Quickly reaching down, Roberta grabbed the stuffed giraffe by the hind leg as Jack's nubby tail wagged vigorously with the excitement and challenge of tug of war. Growling low in his throat, he pressed his paws hard to the carpet, shot his rear end up, and pulled with all his might against Roberta. I love some tug! Jack thought to himself, delighted with this new turn of events, and his stub wagged even more jubilantly as he growled at his new playmate.

Will, meanwhile, had completed the Q and A session and returned, deep in conversation with a tourism professor interested in the topic of space travel. When they opened the door, a small crowd had gathered to watch Roberta engaged in her tug of war with the fearless terrier over the torn, tired, and nonconsenting giraffe.

Recognizing the stuffed animal as her own, the tourism professor joined Roberta in the tug of war. She quickly grabbed for any part of the giraffe she could reach, causing Jack to wag his nub faster and pull with even greater force. Another playmate! I love this UNC place! Squirrels to chase, giraffes to hump, and people that want to play tug! Pressing his paws hard into the carpet again, Jack gave a mighty tug and heard the tear of the leg Roberta was holding.

Jack growled triumphantly and shook the stuffed animal violently from side to side, loosening it from their grips with abnormal strength and speed for his size. I told him to take the game to a more spacious play area and that the main hallway outside would do. Seizing the opportunity, he grasped his hump buddy firmly in his jaws, and dragging part of it on the floor, he darted toward the door that Will was holding open. Will tried to signal to Dowg that it was an ideal time to go, but Dowg was still bent over in tears, sorely incapacitated by laughter.

Chapter 8 - The Death of Sanzio Urban

Yes, it's true, having hump buddies and being oversexed is an important part of our story. If for no other reason, the photographer of the picture died fairly young under fairly similar circumstances, and on his birthday, no less. Known in art circles for putting himself and others into his creative works, you can actually see him there in the picture—I suppose it could be considered something of a selfie. Far right, between the astronomy and theology professors, he is the only one looking directly at the camera. In my opinion, he didn't really deserve to die, but then again, artist types of your kind take little party advice from me, so I'll let you be the judge.

≡Westword

Famed Boulder Artist Sanzio Urban Found Dead: Investigation Underway as Unanswered Questions Linger

The Boulder Police Department and Boulder County Medical Examiner's office have issued statements confirming the death of the notable and well-loved Boulder artist Raymundo Sanzio Urban. Autopsy results revealed that Sanzio died from an adverse drug interaction and dehydration brought on by overexertion related to sexual acts. He was 37 years old. Police and medical services were called to his home in Boulder by Sanzio's partner, Maggie Luti, who claimed that he was unresponsive and did not appear to be breathing. Medical staff were unable to resuscitate Mr. Urban, and he was rushed to Valley Community Hospital where he was pronounced dead at 3:00 am.

According to a statement issued by Boulder Police Department, officials are investigating the claim by Miss Luti that Sanzio was experiencing a fever and that he visited his physician the day before his death. According to Luti, he was prescribed OxyContin for his fever. However, Sanzio's physician has issued a statement claiming that Sanzio came to him with complaints of severe pain, and not a fever, and that he was issued OxyContin. Officials are also investigating the circumstances surrounding his death, including the alleged sex party he attended the night of his death at a property belonging to one Mr. Geoff Stein.

Investigators have questioned Stein about any foul play that may have led to his death, but they have not released any information. Stein was convicted five years ago of having sex with an underage prostitute and for the prostitution of minors. Stein has denied any wrongdoing. Detectives have searched Stein's property and electronic devices and have submitted evidence to the Colorado Bureau of Investigation and the Boulder Police Department. In a joint statement issued by the CBI, the bureau acknowledged that Mr. Stein's email communications with various associates were included in the investigation.

The CBI, in cooperation with the FBI, have evidence to suggest that Stein's email correspondence with several high-ranking government officials, billionaire bankers and financiers contains code words found among pedophiles. In emails obtained by the FBI from Mr. Stein's previous and current investigations, officials still have not determined the context and meaning of the unusual wording in his correspondence among associates.

An anonymous source revealed that the day after the party, where Sanzio is believed to have indulged in drugs and sex just prior to his death, Stein sent an email to another party attendee:

> *"Hi Bill, The realtor found a handkerchief (I think it has a map that seems pizza-related). Is it yours? They can send it if you want. I know you're busy, so*

feel free not to respond if it's not yours or you don't want it."

Mr. Stein could not be reached by **Westword** for an interview to explain the use of the words "handkerchief," "map," and "pizza-related" in the above email or the uses of the words "cheese," "pasta," "ice cream," and "sauce" in previous email communications. The FBI has released information about certain symbols and codes used by pedophile rings and encourages the public to view their website and learn more to help apprehend pedophiles and free children from sex slavery and human trafficking.

FBI officials would not comment on Stein's email language or comment on the sex party and how it may be related to Sanzio's death. Investigators are still exploring whether or not Sanzio saw or knew something that may have made him a target. Could one of Boulder's most beloved and outrageous artist have knowingly or unknowingly stumbled into a pedophile ring?

According to the statement issued by the Boulder PD, officers searched Sanzio's home and found a large art and photography studio in the basement that contained an undisclosed number of past and recent works. Several of the images have been submitted for evidence in two separate investigations.

The first involves images of nude adolescents created for several of Stein's associates that are believed to be involved in pedophilia. However, it is no secret that the talent, creativity and avant garde style of Sanzio Urban was sought after by many wealthy and powerful figures in both political and religious arenas.

The second ongoing investigation involves the continued nationwide manhunt for two *Dyadic Order of Ratio* cult members for high crimes against the US government. Since their failed coup attempt last year in which 22 people were killed, the suspects, known only as Damon and Melissa, have escaped federal authorities. Previous reports suggested that they might be hiding out in the mountains of North Carolina and Tennessee; other witnesses claim that they were seen in the mountains of Utah and Wyoming. The FBI and CBI did not comment on what evidence was found at Sanzio's home, nor how it might be connected to the *Dyadic Order of Ratio*. In a related story, the order's compound outside Boulder was set ablaze in August, and their leader, Paul Guarneri, was shot and killed.

Please contact your local FBI office or submit a tip electronically if you have information involving criminal activity in the deaths of Raymundo Sanzio Urban or Dr. Paul Guarneri or any information leading to the capture of the fugitives Damon and Melissa.

Man hunting. I've participated in many expeditions of this nature, especially when called upon to provide advice for both the hunters and the hunted. I've seen it bring out the best and the worst in men and women, predator and prey alike. Hunting can be intense—it's too extreme for most, especially when they put the hounds on your trail.

Chapter 9 – Hunting with Dowg - September

Dowg's hunting camouflage for September typically included his usual dusty sandals and worn shorts, no need for a shirt. Today, his 50 cent shorts from Goodwill were covered in many white and brown dog hairs and smelled of that peculiar combination of a man's body odor mixed with the scent of a dog—Dowg's typical musk.

"Where do you most like to hunt?" Will asked, still a little unsure of what to expect on his first outing.

"Places of consumption are my favorite," Dowg replied with a twinkle in his eye. "Anywhere there is money, there are rodents, rascals, and scoundrels."

They seated themselves on the Pearl Street Mall in Boulder with their backs against the Wells Fargo mortgage office wall. They were warming themselves in the September morning sun when Will noted a rather obese and seemingly ill-tempered man walk out of the bank with his briefcase.

"Can you give me a few bucks for some food?" Dowg asked, squinting in the sunlight to look up at the man.

"Can you persuade me?" the fat man with the briefcase asked, clearly making a game of the beggar and his simple request. Will watched as the fat man seemed annoyed if not perturbed at having to give any of his time to a homeless man.

Pausing only momentarily to squint again at the heavy man, Dowg said, "If I could persuade you of anything, it would be to hang yourself, you would be doing all of us a favor."

The fat man huffed, seemed about to speak, thought better of it and ambled on down the sidewalk.

Another homeless man, whom Dowg called Lysine for reasons that included peddling crystal meth and other drugs, encountered him on Pearl Street.

"Do you believe in gawd, Dowg?"

Without a moment's pause Dowg said, "Lysine, how can I help believing in a gawd when I see a gawd-forsaken, strung-out, skinny-ass meth-head wretch like you?"

A young adolescent came and sat on a bench near Dowg. As the boy remained glued to his device, clearly playing a video game, Dowg said softly to him, "The better your play, the worse it is for you."

Will and Dowg were still sitting against the wall when another corpulent man, dressed in an expensive suit, walked in their direction.

"Do you mind if we have some of that?"

"Some of what?"

"Some of what's in your pouch."

"I don't have a pouch!" the man replied loudly.

"Sorry about that, thought you had a pouch full of goodies under there," Dowg responded sheepishly, controlling the strong urge to laugh.

The fat man shook his head, muttered something inaudible under his breath, and walked off.

"Behold the fatted sheep wearing an Armani!" Dowg shouted for Will and others within earshot to hear.

"Can you spare a few dollars for some food for me and my dog?" Dowg asked a short, squatty man walking down the Pearl Street Mall.

The man stopped, looked at Dowg, and pondered him for a moment. They stared at each other for a minute, and the squatty man reached slowly for his wallet but then stopped, clearly confused about his decision and taking an abnormal amount of time to act.

"My friend, it's for food that I'm asking, not for funeral expenses," Dowg said with laughter and the usual twinkle in his eye.

A couple and their young son crossed Pearl Street in Dowg's direction. The toddler walking between his parents immediately locked eyes with the beggar sitting on the ground, at his eye level.

"Hey Boy!" Dowg said with an infectious grin and brightness of eyes that halted the toddler.

"Hello, Sir," the toddler responded, still eyed-locked on Dowg, trying to make sense of the energetic and bright-eyed beggar.

Dowg's grin worked its way into an even larger smile when he turned his shining eyes to the father and mother.

"What a pleasant young man!" Dowg said with a delighted satisfaction he rarely showed to others.

"Yes, we are very proud of him," the mother said smiling, looking down at her son who was still eye-locked with the beggar.

"He is also highly gifted," the father replied, "and a very good boy."

"Well then, sounds like he doesn't need me!" Dowg replied with a wink and fist bump to the boy.

By high noon, Wells Fargo security had hassled them off bank property, so Dowg and Will left and headed west toward Settler's Park. Dowg pulled from his grubby shorts his headlamp, which he turned on to its brightest setting, and then strapped onto his head. Coming upon a coffee shop, filled primarily with young people, Dowg entered, walking backwards through the door, then between the tables.

"Can I help you?" an employee of the shop asked.

"I'm looking for some real men," Dowg said, "Have you seen any come in today?"

"I'm not sure what you mean."

"I know. They can be difficult to find these days among the coffee and screen-addicted snowflakes still exploring their gender or someone else's. It's bad enough they are lily-white from a lack of outdoor activity, worse that they are frail and well-intentioned little socialists enslaved by their devices, living off their parents, posing as intellectuals," Dowg said to her softly. Slowly he scanned the room on the off-chance of seeing a man.

"Were there very many men in the coffee shop?" Will asked after Dowg exited the establishment.

"No."

"Where there very many people?"

"Yes."

"I'm looking for an honest man," Dowg replied in answer to the same question from numerous passersby: *What are you doing walking down the street backwards at noon with your headlamp on?*

Doug walked backwards in the hot sun until they came to Settlers Park in Boulder. Coming upon a sandy area off of the Red Rocks Trail, fully lit and heated by the sun's energy, Dowg stopped.

He shed his sandals and then lay down on his back in the hot sand.

Will and two hikers passing by watched Dowg roll in the hot sand from side to side, grunting with the pain of the burning, sunbaked tiny rocks on his bare skin.

"Whatcha doing there, buddy?" one of the hikers asked.

"Worry not friend. It's what I call extreme training," Doug said before turning onto his stomach.

"For what?"

"To make sure I'm tough, in good shape when I have to compete against pleasure and pride."

"For a moment I thought that you were a dog scratching its back," the hiker added.

"You could call me a dog, most do," Dowg replied before rolling over in the hot sand, covering his body and filling his beard with the radiated rocks.

"I'm one of high breed that keeps watch over his friends. I have a habit of barking at dishonest rascals, being friendly with the good, and showing respect for the wise," he said spitting out sand each time he rolled over and said "friend" and "friendly."

And like most any dog would in the heat of the day, Dowg rinsed and cooled off in the shallow September waters of Boulder Creek. It's true, Dowg shared the same fondness for water as did Will. He appreciated this resource as much for survival as recreation, and used it for bathing and fishing. Fish was among his favorite proteins, and he didn't mind consuming it raw.

Chapter 10 – Hopper and Dropper

The most educated of the group on the topic of fresh water fish was indeed Dr. Spencer. His work on the genetic identification of Greenback Trout in Colorado has even stirred controversy among biologists and anglers. Spencer's previous research demonstrated that there were several different strains of cutthroat trout and that some are not even native to the rivers east of Colorado's Continental Divide.

"These include the Greenback, Rio Grande and Colorado River Cutthroat Trout," Spencer explained to Aldo on their walk. For Spencer, the best way to have conversation was while walking.

"Can you refresh me on those scientific names?" Aldo asked, testing Spencer and his reputation as a walking encyclopedia and field guide of the natural world.

"*Oncorhynchus stomias, Oncorhynchus virginalis* and *Oncorhynchus pleuriticus,*" Spencer lisped without delay, hesitation or memory racking.

"Unfortunately, the Yellowfin Cutthroat Trout," Spencer continued, "known as *Oncorhynchus macdonaldi,* went extinct at the turn of the 20th century, shortly after the introduction of the nonnative Rainbow trout." There was a hint of derision in his voice for the distortion of the natural balances of the native fish.

Having departed from the Glen Haven Inn, they crossed the small West Creek Bridge and went right at the Y towards the end of the North Fork Road. With Aldo leading, they came to an unmarked trail that followed the North Fork of the Big Thompson River. This connected with the officially designated US Forest Service trail near the Dunraven Trailhead at an elevation of 7,868 feet. From there, they followed the trail along the well-shaded and tree-strewn stream into the Comanche Peak Wilderness.

Along the road and trail, Aldo had caught six Two-Striped Grasshoppers, *Melanoplus bivittatus* to Dr. Spencer, to preserve the natural purity of the sport of fly-fishing. Where the trail diverged from the stream approximately three miles into the wilderness, they looked down the steep slope of rock and brush to see trout in the deep, unevenly-shaded pools lazily feeding and conserving their energy. Mostly skidding and sliding, they descended the steep embankment to arrive downstream of the deep pools, keeping low and speaking only in whispers.

"If we can see the fish, it's likely they can see us," Aldo said quietly after assembling his fly rod and tying on a very small, bare, size 18 hook. Gently grasping a live grasshopper, Aldo hooked the terrestrial insect neatly and firmly through the thorax. With Dr. Spencer on his left shoulder, he crept forward behind a currant bush, leaving a small patch of unobstructed space for casting with the right hand. The fly reel clicked in consistent compliance at each draw of fly line before Aldo gently false-cast the grasshopper between the bushy banks. Low to the water, he cast sidearm, up the stream, and softly put the grasshopper behind the large rock at the head of the pool.

They watched as the protein-laden insect floated along the top of the pool, flicking and twitching its legs. Aldo, Spencer and I know, as I have told many of your kind; it's all about looking natural. Yes, it's true, I help fish every day distinguish between natural and unnatural foods, and like your kind, being educated makes the difference. Your kind are not their only predators, but you humans educate the trout like few others.

In Colorado, tourists are among the best trout educators. Flinging, slinging, pitching, lobbing and heaving those unnatural smelling globs of bait, lead, and plastic/metallic objects with their many fearsome barbed treble hooks. Perfect for snagging logs, limbs, trees, bushes, tree branches, rocks, nets, dogs, humans, and occasionally, a trout.

On the North Fork of the Big Thompson, the trout have rarely seen much of your kind or the food imitations used for their capture and education. But grasshoppers in the late summer and early fall in Colorado are common. Natural, organic, and non-GMO, they are protein-rich fare for trout in rivers and streams.

A small fish struck at Aldo's grasshopper as it swirled on the water's top toward the right stream bank. Hauling the fly line, he quickly peeled the line up off the water with a sideways back cast -- no fish on, grasshopper still intact. Stopping the rod at the 2 o'clock position on his back cast, he cast forward, stopping at the 10 o'clock position as the line gently laid the insect down, just left of the rock at the pool's head. The grasshopper floated on the swirl of a small eddy towards a grassy and root-bound overhang on the left bank. They could see the flash, then the rise and roll of the fish as the grasshopper disappeared from view on the water's surface.

It occurred to Dr. Spencer that properly setting the hook in a fish is an excellent example of how the mean, or the middle, applies to life. At what time and how much force should be sent through the graphite rod, through the line, to the hook in order to ensure a catch? Too little, too early or too late, the fish will get off, too much force at all, too early or too late, the fish will get off. Seems he has a one in four chance to catch the fish if he is unsure of the mean. Or so Spencer and I reasoned together while Aldo and I focused on timing.

Aldo set the small hook, using the balanced means of both timing and force. With the fly rod tip still held up and sideways, away from trees and bushes, Aldo began gently stripping the fly line while the rod bowed and bounced to the fish's fierce resistance. Keeping the line taut with his right forefinger, Aldo kept his rod tip high, careful not to lose the fish in the roots of the overhang or by the carelessness of having slack in the line.

The trout flashed its steel silver shine, fighting to swim to the safety of the depths of the rooted overhang. Changing direction, it jumped out of the water, shaking its entire body in a tail dance above the eddy's swirling surface. Speeding downstream, along the right bank, the struggling fish went from the head of the pool to the tail. Aldo worked quickly to keep the line taut and out of the branches and bushes.

Stripping the line into two small loops that landed at his feet, Aldo held the bowed rod tip nearly straight up to bring the fish towards him. As it renewed its struggle to swim away, the rod nodded with excitement, and Aldo bent at the knees and then waist to put his free hand in the stream. Gently swishing his submerged hand back and forth with his fingers spread, he tired the fish using the rod's bouncing flexibility with the other hand.

Lifting the wiggling fish slightly out of the water, he gently grasped the slime-covered body with his wet hand and tucked the fly rod between his arm and rib cage. With his right hand free, Aldo gently but quickly removed the small hook from the upper lip of the fish.

"A good looking little brookie," Aldo said softly and opened his hand further for Dr. Spencer to see the eight inch trout.

"Yes indeed," Dr. Spencer said before quickly taking a picture of the fish with his device and recollecting to himself the scientific name to be *Salvelinus fontinalis*. They both briefly feasted their eyes on the beautiful golden underbelly contrasting with the dark green marbling on its back and dorsal fin. On the trout's sides were distinctive red spots surrounded by blue halos.

Aldo then quickly inserted the fish back into the pool with its head facing upstream, gently cradling it so the trout's gills oxygenated its body. After three slow swishes of its tail, the trout regained its energy and darted upstream; two flashes of silver blinking out into the safety of the deep pool's rooted overhang.

"Brook Trout are considered a nonindigenous aquatic species in Colorado," Spencer explained. "I believe that they are originally from the eastern and mid-western U.S.," he added, watching Aldo ready another grasshopper on the small, bare, pure hook.

The remainder of the afternoon was filled with more of the same results with only an occasional hook caught in the bushes and branches. Changing from grasshoppers to small Elk Hair Caddis dry flies, Aldo methodically caught and released trout from the mountain stream. Even Brown Trout, which Spencer photographed and explained to be German invaders, introduced to American rivers and lakes in the late 1800s. They noted the large, dark spotting patterns with red dots, which distinguished it from Brook Trout.

"*Salmo trutta* reside at the top of the trout chain," Spencer explained to our receptive Aldo. "They are strong and aggressive and have outcompeted or simply eaten their native cousins in the U.S., including Colorado," he said observing as Aldo cradled a twelve inch Brown Trout, with its head pointed upstream, recuperating to swim off and live another day among the predators.

Aldo did not catch a Greenback Cutthroat for a photograph and identification. Mostly browns, some brookies, and occasional rainbows, or *Oncorhynchus mykiss* to Spencer.

Aldo grinned from the humor he found in the scientific name-calling of a fish, *mykiss* and unzipped his vest pocket, producing a small fly box. From it, he pulled a small, black flashback, single bead-headed nymph from a rectangular plastic box sectioned by even smaller squares filled with more larva imitations.

"A Two-bit Hooker," Aldo said to Spencer, who noted the small mayfly and stonefly imitation, "it's one I like to frequent in the fall."

Unfamiliar with the common names for wet and dry flies, but familiar with the scientific names ascribed the insects by biologists, Spencer wondered if the common names for flies among anglers could have been derived from pornography star names.

"This time of year, I like a hopper and dropper set up," Aldo stated. "Depending on the river, I've had good luck with Crystal Buggers, Chernobyl Squirrels, Parachute Madam X, Humpy's, Yellow Sallies, Bubble Backs, Soft Hackled Pheasant Tails, and Juju Bees. Some like a Copper John, Fat Albert, San Juan Worm or Stimulator on top. I've had em' take a Scud, Wooly Bugger, Pat's Rubber Legs, and even Rainbow Warriors," Aldo added fingering the various tiny nymphs in the small cubicles of the watertight fly box.

Chapter 11 - WNS - September

In terms of keeping it natural, our kind host at the Glen Haven Inn deals mostly in plants, not animal proteins. We've discussed this notion of keeping it natural, and Anthony and I agree that your kind's relationship with the natural world could accurately be described as one of continued separation, and in more and more cases, irreconcilably divorced. But not for Anthony and Houndman. What Anthony found in gardening naturally lush green kale, chard, spinach, and arugula, Houndman found in smoking wild-caught fish, wild game, and organic tobacco.

When Aldo and Spencer returned to the Inn for WNS, most of the guests had already arrived, and they heard the usual sounds of laughter, clinking glasses and wares. Over the play of Metro's guitar wafted the aroma of Applewood smoke seeping from Houndman's pork-loin-laden smoker. Anthony was working with stuffed portabella mushrooms and green peppers on the grill while he conversed with Zeno, the tall, stone-faced Boulder City Council member.

Dr. Schwede was engrossed in solving a systems engineering problem with Will on his electronic tablet near the cooler of beer where Halsey and Samuel were conversing. Our three graduate students converged at the cooler where Halsey turned to grin at them and open the cooler lid to a host of Colorado libations. Samuel grabbed a Left Hand Brewery Milk Stout, patiently going last as always, and slipped off in the direction of the already engaged Broad and Spencer.

Halsey smiled as he watched Samuel ease his big bulky frame away from the cooler towards the dueling CU and CSU professors.

"Did you know that I wouldn't be here if it wasn't for Samuel?" Halsey said to the students, lifting his beer in the direction of his friend. "He saved my life, not once, but on two separate occasions. You probably didn't know, but Samuel is a decorated US Army veteran. He served in three major US wars in the Middle East, two of them with my unit in Iraq."

"Samuel?"

"Yeah, don't let his soft voice and demeanor fool you; he's tougher than a box of nails," Halsey said, taking a speculative sip of his beer. "We were on patrol near Fallujah, and I was the 50 caliber turret gunner in the lead Humvee. We had turned onto a two-lane road to enter a neighborhood crawling with very bad guys when we ran

107

over a large IED. The explosion killed the soldiers inside and flipped the Humvee upside down, throwing me from the turret onto the roadside."

The students looked at Samuel briefly before reverting their wide eyes back to Halsey.

"Between the explosion and being thrown from the turret, I was disoriented and couldn't see or hear anything except a loud ringing in my ears and some gunfire. I landed on the same side of the road that we were taking fire from in the ambush. I was laying on my back, exposed, and being shot at, trying to get my bearings and hearing," Halsey explained.

"What happened next?" Aldo asked transfixed. He'd had no idea that the two had been in combat together.

"I eventually began to hear the sound of fire from a large machine gun coming closer to me. Lifting my head off the pavement, I could see Samuel running towards me; at the same time, he was sending a long burst of fire from his M240 at the enemy dug in near the road. He grabbed my arm, and we locked our wrists as best I could at the moment. Samuel laid down heavy suppressive fire using his right arm, and by walking backwards, he dragged me out using his left arm. He stayed as low as he could, dragging me across the road into a shallow ditch and never once did he even flinch or ease off the trigger."

The three students looked at Samuel, some distance away, patiently listening to his former student Broad, and Broad's former student Spencer, in discussion. It was difficult for them to imagine the sturdy-framed, soft-spoken family man wielding a heavy machine gun in the heat of combat.

"Look at the guy," Halsey added admiringly. "He's built better than a solid brick shithouse. He can manhandle the M240 with ease, and he is still plenty strong enough to drag my ass out of sticky shit."

Halsey paused momentarily to reflect.

"The second time he saved my life was some years later."

"We were based in Afghanistan with orders to train recruits to fight regimes in the Middle East that opposed U.S. policies. In the live-fire training, an Afghani recruit turned his weapon on the four U.S. advisors training him, including me. Two men next to me were hit, the first one killed and the second one seriously wounded. The shooter missed me and another advisor in the first burst of rounds, so I dove to ground and scrambled for my sidearm while the bastard recovered his aim." Halsey paused and spun the top off a flashy silver flask to pass around the circle of students intently listening.

"Fortunately for me, your average Middle Easterner is a lousy shot, notoriously wasteful with ammunition, and has little tactical sense—unlike Samuel, who with two shots from the tower overlooking the range, ended him, ended it, and saved my ass yet again," Halsey told them, looking fondly at his friend.

"He might not be a gawd's gift to all the good-looking women, but his strength and courage of body and mind are unmatched, whether in a fierce firefight or delicate discussion about logic and living life. He's perfectly content living in a tiny house with a cantankerous woman, which is a Herculean feat in itself. He still works out every day, rarely ever gets sick, and loves to jam out with himself dancing," Halsey said. His admiration and respect were obvious.

"And he could drink any one of us under the table," Halsey added before pausing and grinning.

"Well, there is only one way to find out," said Aldo, grinning back.

Anthony made the call for supper after he extinguished the flames, turned off the gas, and opened the grill lid. To the left of the grill on a table was a large bowl of his freshly-picked kale, chard, spinach, and lettuces in front of various salad dressings, mostly vinegar and oil based. To the right of the grill was the smoker where Dowg was talking with Houndman while he sliced the smoked pork loin to be served.

Will and his peers eventually found themselves in the middle of the line for food, wedged between Dowg and Houndman and the verbally dueling professors, Broad and Spencer. Dowg smiled in eager anticipation to hear their choice of topic.

"As I continue to maintain, the principle of democracy is inherently flawed on several levels," Broad said to Spencer, "A well-ordered state only needs the rulers, the warriors, and the producers who hold all things in common. Children should be raised in common by the state, in which all private property or wealth is common to all. Ideally, officials of the state monitor the talents of the young and…"

Interrupting before Broad could finish his sentence, Dowg barked, "Who brought the tyranny-loving-I'm-smart-enough-to-run-everyone's-lives commie with diarrhea of the mouth?" He smirked at Broad, who shot back his usual frown.

"Pearls to swine is such a waste indeed," Broad replied, loftily.

"I've tried polishing these pearls of yours Broad," Dowg retorted, "and I've come to believe that you have mistaken them for unpolishable turds. The real pearls to be sought are liberty, freedom of speech, and the absence of corrupt and oppressive institutions. The best king is self-rule, not your imaginary one-man do-gooder shat show recipe for group-think and tyranny." Dowg spoke emphatically, his eyes sparkling.

"If I can interject here," Spencer said before proceeding, "Broad's system for a well-ordered state is not aligned with what occurs naturally in humans. The household, not the state, is the first layer of governance, and it is perfectly natural for it to acquire property and wealth. It is also naturally occurring among humans to have a wide diversity of interests, capacities and skills. Broad's system of a well-ordered nation state is unrealistic and clearly smacks of largess in the size and role of government where uniformity and conformity are prized above the individual. It will

112

never last; it's too unnatural," Spencer lisped with consummate confidence.

"I'll drink to that!" Dowg exclaimed before he poured himself a generous glass of wine from the beverage table they had now reached in line.

"What's your favorite wine, Dowg?" Broad asked, jabbing back.

"Whatever you brought," Dowg replied with a bright-eyed smile before moving along to fill his plate, also for free. As you might imagine, free food and beverage matters to Dowg. We could consider it a function of abiding by a simple rule that applies to most homeless men and even bachelors—never turn down a free meal.

Having consumed their fill of supper, Dowg and our graduate students were playing with the dogs on the neatly mowed grass plot adjacent to the Inn. Jack and Pearly were locked in a fierce tug of war over a piece of rope that Dowg had knotted at both ends. Growling ferociously, with his paws planted firmly in the grass, Jack wagged his little nub at each tug by Pearly, manifestly unintimidated by his vastly larger-sized playmate; he didn't let go even when she dragged him halfway across the lawn.

Dowg smiled at the fun-loving little Jack Russell, easily moved by his perpetual displays of courage and utter lack of concern for the size and type of his competition. Reminded of his pleasure in seeing the same in human beings, Dowg went immediately to the topic of *Hunt Club*.

"Will had a small-game outing with me. We didn't even get arrested or beaten up—far too easy of a half day," Dowg said smiling. His message was met with their laughter, especially from Will, as he recalled Dowg's various approaches to effective fat shaming.

Yes, it's true, since our last gathering in Glen Haven for WNS, I've discussed with each of them worthwhile options that fit the criteria of a good prank on deserving persons or organizations relative to their personal causes. As you may recall, the test is that the initiate shows no shame or fear in pulling the prank off, or getting caught, should that happen. To become a club member, the initiate's actions must be witnessed to legitimize and validate a passing or failing grade in embarrassment.

While these *Hunt Club* particulars are important to our story, it is also imperative to understand that there is more to *Hunt Club* than Dowg and Halsey have led the initiates to believe. Dowg has been recruiting for what is the second, known secret society found in the picture. I use the word "known" loosely here for good reasons. Unlike Dr. Guarneri and *The Dyadic Order of Ratio*, individual members of the *Army of the Dog* are not known to the general public nor to local, state or federal authorities as such. *Hunt Club* has become a useful code expression for *Army of the Dog* recruitment and secrecy. Members of the inner semi-circles of the secret society know each other as ADogs and have taken vows to never speak of such in public.

It is highly likely that you've encountered an ADog yourself and didn't know it when you were in Colorado last. Perhaps it was over a simple hello to a passerby walking a dog or two. Maybe it was that person you saw on the river or passed on the trail. It could have been those two graying farmers you saw having coffee or one of those idealism-filled faces you saw in the news demonstrating with home-made signage. Or maybe it's someone that you work with but don't know very well, or perhaps they were those men you saw seated at a tavern disparaging big government institutions and their lies. We all agree: once an ADog, always an ADog.

Halsey kept his word. And with Houndman's help, he had rearranged a table on the deck to accommodate multiple players for a drinking game of *High or Low* between Samuel and our graduate students and any other willing challengers (of which there were none).

"Last man standing," Halsey said with a wolfish grin. Having known Samuel for years, Halsey was confident in predicting the outcome. He took a seat next to Dowg, spun the top off his flashy whiskey flask, and readied himself for the entertainment. With little desire to have a card game dictate how he quenched his thirst, Halsey took a healthy sip from his flask and chased it with a swig of beer.

"Where can I get a pair of shorts like that Metro?" Dowg asked watching Metro walk to and from his car loading music gear.

"Actually, those are called man-capris," Halsey interjected with a slight slur, "notice how they match his man bun?"

"Does Carhartt make a sturdy pair?" Houndman asked joining in, "Those could be useful for cutting firewood if they're strong enough," he added, squinting to better inspect Metro's wear.

"These are called Men's Cropped Capri pants," Metro said looking down at his shorts and smiling. "My girlfriend talked me into them."

"Can she talk you out of them?" Halsey asked, guffawing, "Or do your balls actually breathe in pants that tight?"

"Maybe a pair comes with a free strawberry wine cooler?" Dowg suggested slyly.

Yes, there was plenty of jabbing, bantering, and joking around that Wednesday night as Samuel methodically drank them all under the table. The young men tried valiantly to hold their own, but all were beginning to see double. Slurring as much as he was deliberating on his words, Will asked Samuel what he did for a profession, then belched loudly, and refocused his bloodshot eyes.

"I'm a leadership consultant and life coach," Samuel replied with a smile, clearly unaffected by the alcohol.

"Any chance you can coach Metro out of those sissy britches?" Dowg asked chidingly, "I'd rather see his natural born bare butt than those gawd-forsaken, girly-ass culottes."

Ben bowed out first. After acknowledging his defeat, he careened and stumbled his way with Halsey's help to the nearest chair composing the peanut gallery. Despite their brave and gallant efforts, it was clear that no one, including Will or Aldo would prevail against their burly and unfazed veteran competitor. Samuel could hold own, even in alcohol consumption.

Some made it to their rooms at the Inn, others to their pitched tents, the remainder slept on the deck under the stars, including Ben, Will and Aldo, who passed out in Adirondack chairs. Pearly and Jack lay one on each side of Dowg's nappy old sleeping bag on the deck, Jack mostly inside of it, Pearly pressed against it, covered by Dowg's equally nappy shirt.

As some of you may be aware, I can be very effective or elusive when you are sleeping. Some might even say that I can be confusing when you are dreaming. The dream world is not a place I typically spend much time, but your feelings and fears sure do. It's one of the many unfair advantages my worst enemy – your emotions – has over me.

Like most well-conditioned men of war, Halsey compartmentalized his emotions, and his compartment was plenty full. That Wednesday night, the alcohol-soaked compartment where his war memories were stored, spilled open again.

Yes, it's true. On his first tour in Iraq, they were ordered to open fire on a small white car. It was moving well above the speed limit when it neared a US military checkpoint, and it is still unclear why the confused driver sped directly at the American soldiers. Fearing a suicide car bombing on the checkpoint, Halsey ordered his men to open fire on the vehicle. The hail of automatic weapon rounds riddled the car with large holes, penetrating glass, metal, rubber, flesh and bones. The car veered sharply one way then the other before it crashed into a concrete barrier at the checkpoint's edge.

Inspection of the scene revealed no weapons or explosives in the vehicle. Both occupants had been killed by multiple gunshot wounds to their heads and chests. The driver was a 34 year old Iraqi man and the passenger, his seven-year-old daughter.

In Halsey's dream, she is able to open the car door, and slowly he sees one small foot wearing a pink sandal emerge from the mangled metal onto the pavement. Then the other foot, missing its sandal, also appears. Just as slowly, she stands on one foot, then the other, her small head and torso hidden behind the car door.

Halsey looks about him in his dream to see that no one is there. No soldiers, no civilians, no dogs or even other cars moving on the Iraqi streets and roads. Looking back at the smoking wreckage of the car, Halsey can see that the Iraqi girl has emerged from behind the car door and has stepped towards him.

Halsey sees that her head is lying floppily downward onto her chest. He can see that the right side of her entire face, her neck and the back of her bloodied skull have been grotesquely disfigured by the entries and exits of the many large bullets. Lower on her body, rounds through the chest and shoulder left one arm nearly severed off, dangling by a few small strands of bloody tissue.

Dragging her leg and slightly swinging her nearly-severed arm, she struggles to reach him with her savaged little head still slumped onto her chest. Behind her the car billows with smoke and toxins from the burning wreckage. She drags her leg another step closer to Halsey and tries to extend her one still-intact arm for his help.

Halsey's legs are immovable, like the concrete barrier, firmly fixed to the hot Iraqi pavement. He cannot run to help, or run away, or even run at all.

Reaching him, she stops at his feet with what is left of her small dark-haired head still resting on her bullet-ridden chest. Slowly, and with her one good eye, she lifts her head to look at the tall American soldier. Beginning at his big boots, she works her way up slowly to his torso and automatic weapon. When her eye reaches his eyes, he can see that it is still bright with life but teeming with fear and confusion. It unmistakably without words begs the question of him: *What did I do wrong, American?*

The question travelled at the speed of light from the bright black eye of the disfigured and dismembered girl to rip through Halsey's heart like a perfectly-placed bullet from a sniper.

The still night and beer-induced snores of the Glen Haven Inn and tents pitched nearby were shattered by Halsey screaming. To those awakening to it, it was difficult to discern if Halsey was hollering for his life, or for the life of another, or both. Will and Aldo lifted their beer-fogged heads to see Halsey kicking his legs violently in an attempt to escape his sleeping bag. Pearly, now awakened and on her haunches, looked towards Halsey and gave a low, deep growl, unsure of the situation or assailant. Jack jumped out of the sleeping bag and barked loudly at the invisible intruder until Halsey was awakened abruptly from his night terror.

After I told him where he actually was and was not, Halsey regained himself and lay down on his back; his chest heaved with deep breaths that sounded like deep sighs. When his breathing slowed and his body relaxed, Pearly approached him timidly with her tail wagging gently. Halsey didn't resist her when she licked his face or touched his ear with her soft, wet nose. Removing any trace of tears, Pearly laid down next to him and pressed against his side. Halsey laid his arm on her, his hand gently petting her neck while they shared their warmth and she shared her calm.

"It's too damn unnatural," Dowg muttered softly to himself and the little terrier as he nestled his way back into the sleeping bag with Dowg. "War isn't our kind of hunting, little buddy."

Chapter 12 - The Nature of Efficiency – Gym Lesson 2

"It's all about reading the natural signs," Houndman said. "No different than reading the line on the river or on the mountain bike trail or in the pursuit of a wise and beautiful woman—one must pick a line, Will."

Will had chain-sawed a good deal of Houndman's log pile by mid-September. No major injuries aside from landing a large round on his foot, smashing his thumb, and slipping off the logs twice. Pleased with progress, and ready to change metallic weapons, Will decided to split some rounds of firewood.

"For splitting, nature has already provided the lines to us," Houndman said, pointing to three cracks in a dry round of Douglas fir, "and they are our targets for the ax, maul or wedge."

"Think efficiency through accuracy and finesse," Houndman instructed, "use brute force only when necessary; you'll conserve energy and save your back."

Seizing another chance for an analogy, Houndman continued. "Stay on target. It's better to swing softly and hit the crack than to swing with great force and miss it. Focus on accuracy and reliability in your swing; anything else would be inefficient and wasteful," he explained. "And be sure to split around, not through, the knots," he added before he reached for the eight-pound splitting maul propped against a nearby round.

With his left foot slightly in front of his right, Houndman raised the heavy splitting maul past his right shoulder into the air high over his head until the metal head was momentarily suspended near the apex of the swing. With his thick, mountain-man beard buried in the crux of his left bicep and forearm, he slipped his right hand to the base of the handle to meet his left hand. With eyes locked onto the crack in the round, Houndman contracted his abdomen and sent the energy through his arms and wrists to the handle accelerating the steel head.

With seemingly little effort, Houndman sent the metal maul at high speed deep into the targeted crack. Will felt the energy of the swing disperse through the ground as the loud and deep report of the separating and tearing wood ricocheted off the nearby rocks as a low cracking thud. With a second swing of even less effort, the round split open and lay in halves, each scenting the morning air with the fragrance of fresh fir meat.

"Uh Oh! Did Broad fall and hit his head?" someone asked loudly, "I thought I heard a hollow thud back here!"

Looking up, they saw Dowg laughing and walking toward them, followed by Jack and Pearly. Met by Houndman's old white hound Cassee, the dogs completed their greeting niceties of sniffing, nose bumps, licking and tail wagging.

Cassee did not overlook Dowg; instead she approached him to sit down at his feet and extend her paw for his arm and a grasp. Jack wagged his little nub in the furious delight of being among good friends, primed for the prospect of new adventures. Practically dancing with excitement, Jack stopped to stand on his back legs to paw at Houndman's thigh and look intently into the mountain man's eyes.

"Which do you find most preferable Dowg, humans or dogs?" Houndman asked smiling into Jack's little eyes and scratching the back of his little ears.

"No brainer—it's clearly dogs," Dowg replied playing along. "Their worth is more than the lives of any given number of humans," he added with a smile and a pet of Ol' Cassee's neck.

Still listening to Houndman and Dowg, Will picked up the splitting maul and took a hard swing at the crack in the pine round. He missed. The heavy maul head bounced back up and sent vibrations from the maul handle through his hands to the base of his back ending at the bottom of his feet.

"In terms of living efficiently, dogs are far superior to humans on nearly every level. Even in living a natural and simple life with few needs outside of the very basics. Hands down, dogs are more highly evolved beings," Dowg stated with supreme confidence, noting that Will had missed the crack and was taking another swing.

"It should be blatantly obvious to any observer of dogs that they are superior in their abilities to adapt to varying circumstances, to operate with absolute honesty, and to exercise their right to freedom of speech by saying whatever to whomever whenever and however," Dowg continued, "These virtues and strengths deserve to be respected and imitated by the drastically inferior humans".

Will took another swing with the splitting maul. Missing again to the opposite side of the crack, the metal head bounced off the top of the pine round once again, sending a shudder through his body. He swung again and missed again and buried the maul head in the fleshy meat of the pine round to no effect.

"Worry not Will. Nothing in life has any chance of succeeding without strenuous practice, for it alone is capable of overcoming anything," Dowg said, smiling encouragingly.

Keeping his eye on the intended crack that was the target, Will was raising the splitting maul over his head again for his next swing when a loud commotion of flapping wings and squawking echoed from the hen house.

"Jack!" Houndman hollered.

"Easy, Killer!" Dowg shouted, trying to conceal his smile.

Will set the maul down and ran towards the cackling hens, flying feathers, and the speedy Jack Russell, his nub wagging furiously with delight. Before they could reach him, he pounced on one of the hens, working quickly to find holds with his paws and jaws. Her squawking turned into screeching and a flurry of flapping, and feathers enveloped Jack in a small cloud, some floating gently down on the morning air.

Having subdued the chicken with his paws and body weight, Jack placed his jaws on the back of her neck. His nubby tail had slowed to a more constrained, methodical and rhythmical wag at the same time we strategized how to elude his oncoming opponent. Hearing me, Jack sped up the wag of his tail to the high frequency of a game of keep away with the struggling chicken in his jaws. Leading Will to the corner of the coop, Jack quickly juked and shot past him through the open gate to display his predator prowess to Dowg and Houndman.

Strutting with his head high as the chicken struggled, flapped and squalled in his small, strong jaws, Jack made several passes by the laughing men, parading on the tree bark floor of the *Swift Dog Gym*. Still laughing himself, Will watched Jack gently let go of the chicken as soon as Houndman bent over to grab her from him. Without running off, Jack looked up into his eyes, pressed his ears back and wagged his tail for confirmation from Houndman with the unmistakable look of *What? That's not good fun?*

Dowg watched as the hen, with much clumsiness and lopsided lumbering, broke into an awkward sprint using claws and wings to propel her back to the safety of her cackling coop mates.

"Does that chicken remind you of anybody, Houndman?" Dowg asked wiping his eyes, mostly recovered from his laughter.

Houndman thought for a moment.

"Maybe if it was featherless?"

Chapter 13 - A Color Run – Dowg Interrogation #1

Seated next to the entrance of the Target department store on Pearl Street, Dowg warmed himself in the mid-morning sun, observing the hustle and bustle of passersby. He watched as a poor, young adolescent boy emerged from the store and was quickly approached by a Target asset protection specialist that had followed him out.

"Mind if we have a quick conversation?" the protection specialist asked the boy, flashing his badge discreetly in the palm of his hand for the adolescent to see. Clearly surprised but saying nothing, the boy stepped to the side of the exit with the specialist near where Dowg was sitting and watching. The officer asked the boy to produce the contents of his hooded sweater pocket front, which he did, yielding a small plastic container of chocolate milk.

Dowg watched as the young boy fought back tears and bit his quivering little lip. With one hand firmly on the boy's shoulder and the other holding a radio device to his lips, the asset specialist escorted the boy towards the main office.

"Look everyone!" Dowg shouted loudly as he stood up and pointed his middle finger at the asset specialist, "Watch the big thief take away the little thief!"

"All hail the big thief!" Dowg yelled for all in the vicinity to hear and to look his way. Pausing, Dowg bent over and waved his arms in the most sarcastic royal bow he could muster.

Having gained the attention of a small group outside the store, including some shoppers in the parking lot, Dowg got down on his knees and raised both of his arms above his balding head, his eyes gazing upward at the heavens.

"All praise be to the corporate thieves!" Dowg wailed before throwing his arms and face down onto the sidewalk in total submissive worship. Pausing only momentarily, he again threw his face and arms skyward in earnest prayer.

"May every young person living with hunger be denied by our corporate masters! Oh Great Gawd Almighty! Have mercy on our corporate slaveholders and shareholders!" Dowg wailed as he bowed his face and arms humbly onto the concrete sidewalk in front of the large Target sign and symbol.

Upon the completion of his "prayers," Dowg sat down again at his vantage point to watch, wait, listen and exercise his rights to free speech. He soon noticed an especially obese man enter the store in an undersized t-shirt emblazoned with an American flag and the words, *"These Colors Don't Run."*

"There is an honest shirt that matches the fat beast wearing it," Dowg thought to himself before he stood up and followed the large man into the store. After taking a moment to scan the store for the asset protection specialists, the spectacle of shoppers, and the signage, Dowg made his way to the sporting goods section. First, he found a biking helmet, then a pair of boxing gloves, and last he selected a graphite *Mongoose* bike for teens with 20" x 4" supersized tires. He raised the seat, put on the helmet and gloves, and hopped on the bike.

Dowg pedaled slowly towards the main aisle where he yelled, "Fire!!!" at the top of his lungs.

"Fire!!! Fire!!!" Dowg cried. He turned onto the main aisle and stood up on the bike pedals for more speed and a better view of the shoppers' reactions. Biking towards the main aisle at the front of the store, Dowg watched as most of the astonished faces looking at him turned and ran for the doors, many with items still in their hands, which set off the alarm system upon exit. Dowg turned left into the main aisle shouting his life-saving warning until he reached the main exits, where he coasted to a stop to watch the mayhem gain momentum.

From his vantage point on the seat of the kid's bike, Dowg was able to identify the honest men and women. That is, the ones who were interested in knowing where the fire was and what needed to be done to put it out.

"There's one," Dowg said several times out loud as he pointed to various people exhibiting the reaction he most respected. This confused the shoppers even more, thinking that he was pointing out the fire's location.

"Where? I don't see any smoke?" someone asked frantically.

"Exactly," Dowg replied sporting a large grin. "The honest aren't engulfed in smoky illusions."

Dowg's highest satisfaction was realized when he watched the large man with the shirt *These Colors Don't Run* running, as best he could, for the door and his life. Content with having performed for this man, and many others, a necessary service, Dowg noted between tears of laughter, a Target manager and asset specialist approaching him.

He wiped his eyes and could see that it was the same man who had caught the boy stealing the milk. Dowg saw that the boy had been ordered to follow behind the asset specialist while the employee attempted to make sense of the mayhem created by the helmeted homeless man on the kid's bike, wearing boxing gloves and yelling about a fire.

Without hesitating, Dowg pushed the bike forward with his feet and pedaled furiously away from the asset specialist and the boy with him. Yes, it's true, I told the boy it was a good time to run away when the specialist began to pursue the laughing, helmeted, bearded man weaving in and out of the fleeing shoppers.

"Fire!!! Fire!!!" Dowg yelled again loudly, speeding in and out of the aisles to confuse the growing number of pursuers after him. Their running steps echoed like pounding infantry boots in the nearly empty store. Mostly cornered in the front of the store opposite the exit, Dowg soon reached the end of the main aisle. He turned and looked to see several men, some in security uniforms, running toward him from the opposite end of the main aisle.

Wasting no time, Dowg stood on the pedals and pumped them feverishly in the direction of the men. The *Mongoose* kid's bike groaned and flexed under the adult weight as Dowg picked up speed, quickly closing the gap between himself and the men who seemed less and less sure what to do. On the timing of my command, Dowg grasped the right brake lever firmly with his boxing glove and locked the fat back wheel into a controlled skid.

The squealing rubber on the polished floor left a long black stain even when Dowg leaned the bike hard to the left and glided, his left foot dragging along the floor. At nearly full speed, Dowg laid the bike down and sent it sailing knee high at the men running at him. Clad in the safety of his helmet and boxing gloves, he slid with his bike into the men, upending them and a large cardboard display case of Denver Bronco bobble-head figurines.

Upon completion of gravity's work, the flurry of arms, legs, pot bellies and security badges came to rest mostly on top of Dowg. Yes, it's true, this was not the first time Dowg had put himself into a situation where he would be handled roughly if not thrashed thoroughly. He considered these friendly scrimmages to be the stuff of good fun, necessary action, and worthwhile exercise. This unique and superior form of cross fit training is actually a hallmark workout for *Swift Dog Gym* members, even at Wal-Marts.

Dowg was curled in a ball when the punching and grappling ensued. With his head mostly protected by the bike helmet, he put his boxing gloves to his cheek bones to shield his face from the blows. In my opinion, Dowg's fun scrum would have been much shorter-lived if he hadn't been laughing so hard at his assailants. The more they tussled, cussed and fussed, the harder Dowg giggled, laughed and howled among the bouncing, bobble-headed Broncos scattered about the aisle floor. On his way out of the Target, Dowg danced like a boxer and sang to his escort, following along loudly with the store's sound system, still playing but nearing the end of a poor Muzak version of *The Eye of the Tiger*.

The boy who had stolen the chocolate milk had not run far away from the store. He was positioned across the street behind a car, well away from the main exit to see what would become of the homeless man. The boy soon saw the still-singing Dowg and his entourage of police officers and asset specialists and noted that Dowg had been handcuffed and his helmet taken away, but he was still wearing boxing gloves.

Stepping out quickly from behind the car, the little boy made a fist with his right hand and pumped it into the air for Dowg to see.

Dowg caught his fistful of message and smiled from ear to ear before shooting him a wink and a nod.

Can we recruit boys that young into *Hunt Club*? Dowg asked himself in consultation with me as they sat him down on the noticeably comfortable seat of the police car.

At the Boulder police station, Dowg waited impatiently for nearly two hours as officers, many whom he recognized from previous encounters, and administrative assistants went about their work at varying speeds. Every so often, he lifted one of his sturdy butt cheeks to let fly a lengthy and noisy fart. The woman at the desk glanced at Dowg over the top of her glasses and frowned, shaking her head. After the third deadly release of methane gas tainted with the smell of raw fish and kimchi, she left her desk.

Bored again, Dowg decided to practice whistling a version of *The Eye of the Tiger* to soothe his impatience and aggravate his captors until an officer escorted him to a small room with a large one-way viewing window. He was still whistling when a tall and rather sturdy investigator with neatly-cropped brown hair and a file folder entered the big-windowed interrogation room.

"Douglas Snopes," the officer said without pausing, "I'm Special Agent H. Mortimer Bennett with the Colorado Bureau of Investigation."

"Is that H. for Humper?" Dowg asked nonchalantly before considering the agent's employer. "The Colorado Bureau of Investigation?" he said, surprised, "Am I finally being honored for the high crime of fat-shaming shoppers and having them exercise some?" Getting no reaction from Bennet, he continued. "Is there a ceremony?" he asked with nearly untraceable sarcasm, staring defiantly into the steady eyes of the investigator.

Without answering, Special Agent Bennett opened a file and selected an oversized document, which he unfolded from its halves and placed on the table in front of Dowg.

"Are you in this photograph, Doug?"

Dowg looked at the picture for some time but did not respond. Even upon further inspection of the picture and a summons for me, he was unable to make sense of all the images in it. But this did not diminish the simple fact that yes, he himself was in the picture, a little below and slightly right of center, in the blue, lying on the steps reading.

"Can you believe it, Mortimer?" Dowg said loudly with as much sincerity as he could muster. "The Colorado Bureau of investigation has successfully solved a mystery, but no crime! Yes, that's me in the photograph. And I have to admit that the entire picture would be improved if my dogs were in it as well."

"Do you know anyone in this photograph, Doug?"

Dowg paused briefly and continued to inspect the picture. "I know some. I know some well. I know who some are, some I've never met before, and some I've never seen before," he replied.

Seizing upon this affirmation, Investigator Bennett explained that the pending loitering, assault and property damage charges against Dowg would be dropped contingent on his cooperation and confidentiality in the conduct of a federal investigation.

"A federal investigation?" Dowg inquired with some surprise and as much curiosity. "Which tyrant corporation would this involve? Do you have a handler I should know about? Is he looking at me from the one-way window?" He pointed to it with his middle finger.

Having been warned already by Boulder PD about Dowg's obstinance, Bennett stayed the course with his questions. "Do you know who took this photograph?"

Dowg flipped the picture over to inspect the blank back side, then flipped it back over to examine the front again, looking carefully along the edges.

"I don't see a name anywhere on it," he answered sardonically, having no idea who took it.

"Can you tell me anything about the context of the photograph?" Bennett asked, his annoyance well-hidden, his gaze still steady.

"Maybe," Dowg said, looking at the picture and conversing more with me about the anomalies in it. "This picture was taken at CU during *Weekly Seminar* at the Mary Rippon Outdoor Theater."

"*Weekly Seminar?*"

"*Weekly Seminar* is a consortium of professors and graduate students from various institutions of higher education found on Colorado's Front Range. At any given seminar at CU Boulder, faculty and students from CU, CSU, UNC—that's C for Cowshat—not Carolina, Metropolitan State University of Denver, and Denver University are in attendance," Dowg explained.

"What do they do at this seminar?" Bennett inquired.

"Occasionally it's informative, but it's mostly pissing matches among egos. They meet to present and discuss all things related to their academic boastings about their research, grant writing, articles, and books."

"Why would a homeless man such as yourself attend an academic meeting with professor types?"

Dowg laughed. Somewhat for the reason that the investigator didn't know why he had chosen homelessness for himself, but mostly from the comedy that Dowg derived from thinking about academics in higher education.

"I've learned a great deal from several of these men, including Broad there," Dowg explained. "And when he isn't making sense, I'll counter him at every opportunity, because few others will."

"Broad?"

"Broad is the wackjob mystic fraud there, just left of center with his index finger pointing up," Dowg said imitating the same gesture except crossing his eyes, stroking his chin, and distorting his face into his most intellectual pose. "Upward to La La land, where bizarre forms, nutty rituals, unhinged abstractions and other such quackeries roam freely in and out of his brain."

Dowg seemed pleased to finally elicit something of a smile from the investigator, given his attempts at humor. "Do babies usually attend?" Bennett asked before he pointed to the leftmost bottom corner of the picture.

"Aside from Broad and his camp? No, babies don't attend," Dowg said shaking his head and looking more closely at the picture. "I have no idea how this baby ended up in the picture. Or who that boy might be? Or the woman in the white for that matter..." He paused. "Is that a woman?" he asked, still scrutinizing the picture closely with a puzzled look.

"Are you acquainted with any of these individuals in the lower-left corner surrounding the big balding man with the beard and the book?" Bennett asked, pointing to them and looking at Dowg for his response.

It was then that I first convinced Dowg that the picture he was looking at had been manipulated by the photographer. You may have already deduced that the chronology of their lives is demonstrably out of order in the picture. Yes, it's true, the picture was not simply taken at one point in time as it would appear; it's actually a collection of superimposed images from different *Weekly Seminars,* taken over the years, at the same Mary Rippon Outdoor

Theater. These were then cleverly photo shopped by the creator.

"How is possible," Dowg asked, "that Dr. Guarneri, who hasn't attended *Weekly Seminar* in years, and who was shot and killed in early August, can appear in a photograph that was taken in September?" Dowg was still confused by the images.

"How do you know it's a recent photograph?"

"You see that little Peter Pan beta boy there next to me with his back to the camera—that's Metro, our effeminate libtard punching bag. He's a music student at CU," Dowg explained. "Nice kid, but hopelessly confused."

"What did you say to him at the time?" Bennett inquired. "He seems upset with you."

"Metro was in another one of his effeminate drama queen modes at the start of this seminar, and it got on my nerves, no more than usual, really, but I was trying to read. I may have said something to the effect of '*It's bad enough that nature had you born a man, no need to make matters worse by acting like a woman,*'" Dowg recollected.

"What were you reading when the picture was taken?"

"Likely *The Wall Street Urinal,*" Dowg replied, squinting for a closer look at the picture, "or maybe it was the *Washington ComPost,*" he tried to recall, "but for certain a corporate publication I retrieved from a campus recycling bin, meaning it's one a professor would read." He added with a grin, "I'm compulsed to keep watch, like a guard dog, and read the lies they read and believe and pass onto the young."

Agent Bennett stared at Dowg for a moment, considering a more direct approach. "Are you aware of any secret society activity surrounding *Weekly Seminar*?"

Without hesitating, "I figured you know more than I about Paul Guarneri and the *Dyadic Order of Ratio*. After all, wasn't it federal agents that shot him in the back after setting fire to their compound?" Dowg asked, taking his turn to observe how Investigator Bennett might field a question himself.

The investigator neither answered it nor did he hesitate. "What can you tell me about Guarneri and his influencing young people to follow him in a secret society?" he asked pointing to Damon and Melissa in the picture. You can see them there in the picture in the bottom left corner. Melissa is holding a tablet next to Guarneri, and appears to be communicating with Damon, who is mostly hidden behind the pillar.

"I've heard his band *Tetractys* play in Central Park," Dowg replied, "all originals—no covers— pleasantly relaxing jam band music in my opinion. Seem like mostly laid-back hippy types to me, and they don't tend to jabber on about nothing between songs. From what I've seen, they are eager to avoid conflict or harm, and seem happy enough playing around with music and geometry. I find it difficult to fault anyone who has decided to drop out of this society. This circus of dishonest institutions governed by insatiable greed, so that they can keep to themselves, eat healthy foods, and contribute no harm," Dowg concluded.

Before Bennett could follow up, Dowg launched into his fondest recollection of Guarneri and one of Dowg's many encounters with Boulder PD. Before Guarneri dropped out and could still be seen in public, he was in Boulder and came upon a loud commotion on his walk by Central Park. Hearing the sounds of struggle and loud squalling combined with blood curdling screams, Guarneri sprinted in the direction of the howls for mercy.

Guarneri entered the park on the Boulder Creek Path and nearly collided with an animal control officer attempting to subdue a large, long-legged hound dog squalling for its life. At the same time, Dowg was in a struggle to free his dog from the other animal control officer. All this without wearing boxing gloves or a helmet.

Seeing Guarneri come upon them, his face racked with anxiety and alarm, the officers stopped and looked at him, unsure of what he might do.

"Easy, gentlemen!" Guarneri said loudly between deep breaths. "Easy! That wailing dog sounds like the voice of an old friend of mine!" he pleaded. Strangely, he was nearly in tears, his eyes locked on the wild eyes of the heavily panting hound.

Guarneri's respect for dogs and for animals in general was well-known. Some have even asked me if it is possible that he could communicate with animals. He was also held in very high regard by nearly everyone at *Weekly Seminar*, including Broad and Spencer. Indeed, Spencer even shared some of the same opinions as Guarneri and his followers. Yes, it's true, I convinced Dr. Spencer that Guarneri was actually a rare convergence of reincarnations, in which that large brain of his housed the memories and experiences of multiple lives lived before him.

Strange, I know, not what you might expect from Spencer. But what is for certain, I convinced Guarneri long ago that to live a virtuous life is to be at harmony with the universe. The same chord I struck with nearly every thinker in the picture, even Dowg, who didn't feel the least compelled to disparage a man of virtue before an officer of the law.

"When I think of violent revolution, the first image to come to my mind is a bunch of dignified pacifists keeping to themselves. Maybe munching on some raw vegetables, absorbed in their music, math and harmony?" Dowg suggested sarcastically. "I've never met Guarneri's students, and it still doesn't make sense to me how they could have been influenced to attempt such acts of courage and violence between songs at band rehearsal or pulling weeds from the garden; it just doesn't make any sense to me."

"Can you tell me about the Arab man who seems so interested in what Guarneri is reading?" Bennett asked.

Dowg looked at the bottom left corner of the picture at the man leaning over Guarneri's left shoulder, with his head and headwear tilted sideways, his right hand over his chest.

"That's would be Dr. Averroes; he's a professor of Middle Eastern Studies, a physician and big fan of Spencer's, actually. He's also written extensively on the relationship between philosophy and religion, especially Islam."

"Are you aware of any connections that Averroes might have with foreign or domestic terror organizations?" Bennett inquired.

Dowg laughed before answering, his eyes twinkling. "The only terror he's ever caused was probably in the brains of some faith-headed rednecks in Afghanistan and neighboring Pipelineistan. He's renowned for bringing hardcore fringe elements of religions together to re-visit and re-reason violent and irrational belief systems. Like a missionary, but for reason and peace. You might want to keep your eye on him; the warmongers wouldn't want a dreadful peace to break out in such a time of so many blissful wars."

Bennet shook his head. Sometimes he had a hard time following Dowg's answers. He plowed on. "And who is this man?" Bennett asked pointing to the image in the lower left corner of the picture: a man in yellow holding a book, with his foot propped up, his eyes on Guarneri.

"That would be Dr. Parmen," Dowg answered. "Whom I never met before," he added, "but I understand that he was a professor of philosophy and logic at CU and was among the first to pose good questions about the nature of reality. His conclusions to these questions, and the refutations that followed them, especially those posed by H.L. Michaelsen, are still fun for thinking types to ponder."

"H.L Michaelsen?"

"Yes, people who know him well call him Cletus. He's there, leaning his elbow on the table next to Dr. Parmen," Dowg said pointing to the muscular, melancholy man in the picture. "We don't see much of him; he takes to the woods most of the time—isn't exactly fond of his fellow human beings, and who could possibly blame him?"

"What is it about the nature of reality that Dr. Parmen and Cletus disagreed on?" Bennett asked with diminishing hope of finding any sort of connection with the fugitives.

This question rekindled the spark in Dowg's eyes as he considered a succinct reply.

"Parmen's view was that reality is a fixed and unchanging entity, and Cletus's view was that reality is a dynamic, constantly changing entity, like each step in the moving waters of a river. Which begs a good question, Mortimer," Dowg suggested with some authority. "Is reality constantly staying the same or is reality constantly changing?"

It occurred to Bennet later that evening when he was pondering Dowg's question over a macrobrew, that he'd forgotten to ask the question *what is our reality*?

Chapter 14 - Hunting with Dowg –Buffaloes in October

Like many of the dichotomies created in those large but underutilized brains of yours, the answer to an otherwise simple question can be complicated by the artificially created demarcation line itself. Is it possible that it is both constantly the same and constantly changing? If what you call "reality" is a function of evolutionary processes, could it be reasoned that nature's laws do not change but that the natural world is constantly changing?

For example, consider the many sports of your kind, such as the Olympic Games. Much has stayed the same while much has changed. From track and field, to curling and snowboarding, to ping pong. Even within that violent but highly entertaining sport of American football, the rules are mostly the same, but the players are changing, one brain or body injury at a time.

As for dogs and their ancestral alpha parent wolves, lying in the warmth of the morning sun on a cool October morning hasn't really changed over time despite ever more selective breeding. Dowg was also found quite often sunning himself on cool mornings, leaning against the large plastic tub that served as his tent in Central Park. Our three graduate students came upon him and saw that he was reading yesterday's newspaper. Dowg looked up as they approached, his eyes bright with vigor.

"Let's get after it boys!" Dowg quickly tided up his tub. "It's another football Saturday! He snickered. "Plenty of mindless rascals misspending their lives on useless diversions!"

"Why do you even go to football games, Dowg?" Will asked, well into their stroll to the stadium.

"For the simple reason that I see myself competing side by side with the athletes, only my competitors and hardships are far fiercer than their artificial ones," Dowg answered.

"Why do you think athletes are often perceived as being simple or slow-minded?" Ben asked.

"Because they are mostly meatheads built of beef and pork."

"Who do you find to be among the most intelligent people in society?" Aldo asked.

"Physicians, philosophers and pilots, among others," Dowg replied.

"Who do you find to be the most silly? Will inquired.

"The whole range that includes rich and conceited pricks and dream-interpreting psycho-babbling mystics and artist types, lost in their abstractions and feelings," Dowg answered without hesitation.

They arrived at the CU Buffaloes game at Folsom Field in Boulder. Dowg positioned himself where he could overlook the tunnel from which the football players emerged. He scanned their large, armor-covered bodies and helmeted heads and watched them work themselves up by jumping up and down, dancing, and hollering in excited anticipation of the game.

"I see nothing but smoke!" Dowg shouted at the players waving his hand to clear the imaginary particles from his vision. "Argh, the smoke!" he shouted again and coughed to clear his lungs. "Nothing but smoke!"

Seeing an extremely large and fit athlete casting repeated glances at a beautiful young woman waving at him, Dowg pointed and proclaimed loudly, "See! A buffalo frenzied for battle, yet is held fast by the neck, captivated by a common pussy cat!"

"Everywhere I look, all I see is smoke!" Dowg shouted to the roaring crowd.

Yes, it's true, Dowg shouted at the crowd about smoke well into the 2nd quarter. He even touched on his least favorite industrial complexes, tyrant corporations and societal institutions, including higher education and sports in higher education.

"Damn smoke everywhere!" he shouted, waving his hands, coughing and squinting at the crowd.

"Too bad these brutes strive so hard to outdo each other in football," Dowg said when a touchdown was scored, "when they could be striving to be good and honest men instead."

"What do you mean Dowg?" Will replied, "The NFL is known for their good and honest men."

"Isn't that the acronym for the National Felons League?" Dowg queried, "Or is that Not For Long?"

"You don't hate all people, do you, Dowg?" Ben asked.

"No, I don't hate all people, but I hate it when evil people are consumed by their moral depravity, and I hate it even more when good people do nothing in the face of evil and moral depravity."

"Look around us," Dowg continued. "Look at these people." He pointed to the many faces in the stadium. "Look at them go through great pains and emotional upheavals for their team to win, when in reality, they would be much better off without this contrived game inaccurately called football."

Despite his shouting, heckling and gesturing during the football game, Dowg, to his profound pleasure, was unable to embarrass our three graduate students with his antics. Past the midpoint of the 4th quarter, they left their seats so that Dowg could position himself outside of the main exit, on the stadium's east side.

He retrieved a headlamp from a pocket of his dog-hair-covered pants, set it on the flashing red strobe mode, then strapped it to his balding head. Facing the afternoon sun, Dowg walked backwards through the exit area as the crowds spilled out from the stadium.

Jostled by the continuous bumps, pushes and nudges against the back of his shoulders, the beggar with the head lamp stopped and looked at and over the faces surrounding him.

"I can't see through all the meatheads and their arm candy!" Dowg shouted.

"What are you looking for?" someone asked.

"*An honest man*! All I see are those more alive to their dreams of winning a silly game than to their real lives! Where did all the real men go?" Dowg asked while the red strobe of the head lamp rhythmically pulsed onto the confused and annoyed faces of the football fans.

Chapter 15 – Big Bank Deposit

Regardless of which norms you or society's institutions may or may not apply to discern a real man, Dowg was steadfastly unwavering in the criteria he applied. This was no less so than with *Hunt Club* initiations. Pass or fail is contingent on the following: not displaying embarrassment or a flushed red face, no nervous non-verbal body language, or speaking in choppy and incoherent sentences if confronted by strangers or security. Yes, it's true, I convinced all three of our graduate students to take Dowg's manliness test for *Hunt Club* membership, beginning with trifecta-recovering Will. His soul-hole for Kota was healing slowly with time, and he was rather enjoying his earthen den and duties at Houndman's. But Will's dad, Guy Fiedler, was still embroiled in his fight with Wells Fargo. *He* didn't mind sleeping in the shop with a shotgun nearby, but it sorely worried Will's mother.

Dressed in the camouflage of the finest dark-blue suit he could find that morning at Goodwill, and with his blonde hair carefully combed to the side and slicked back, Will bore a cleverly-made name tag reading ***Richard DePore***, and in smaller letters below, ***US Federal Reserve Bank***. Armed with a sturdy and well-functioning mega horn, he and Dowg rounded the corner of Broadway Boulevard in Denver on their way to the main branch of Wells Fargo & Company. They had considered smaller branches of the bank elsewhere on The Front Range, but Dowg decided to go big, to the main branch.

When they arrived, Will set the bullhorn down momentarily and took several deep breaths. He leaned over slightly and shook his arms and hands like a swimmer loosening up for a big event before picking up the bullhorn and putting it to his mouth.

"Testing. Testes. Testing," Will said into the bullhorn in front of the mammoth bank building. Dowg had found a comfortable place to watch from the large, long stone steps of the bank's entrance. With his eyes mostly on Will, Dowg felt confident that his first initiate would not succumb to that hideous form of embarrassment where a man cares more about what others think of him than he cares for the Truth.

"Dick DePore here!" Will blasted over the megaphone in a commanding voice. "Denver Branch of the Federal Reserve Bank of Kansas City," he announced to better the sell and gain the attention of the creditors and depositors coming and going.

"Please do not panic, ladies and gentlemen!" he bellowed in his deepest, most official-sounding voice. "The Wells Fargo bank will be closing today at noon sharp. I repeat, this bank will be closed at noon today—please do not panic!" he said as calmly as possible before instructing anyone within hearing distance to immediately transfer or withdraw their funds from Wells Fargo.

To Dowg's delight, the confusion turned to panic on the faces of some, but mostly disbelief on those faces late to hearing Will's bad, good news. Dowg watched on as Will took a question between blasts of the bullhorn, urging them to immediately withdraw their funds from the big bank.

"What happened?!" Will asked over the bullhorn, echoing a question from a bystander in the crowd.

"I'll tell you what happened!" His loud voice boomed off the walls of the bank.

Will produced a somewhat small, but rather official-looking leather-bound memo from his shirt pocket. Quickly flipping it open, Will read over the bullhorn the following fines applied for crimes committed by Wells Fargo:

- $175 million for discrimination against African-American and Hispanic mortgage borrowers

- $6.5 million for not disclosing the risks associated with mortgage-backed securities
- $42 million for neglect of foreclosed homes in African-American and Hispanic neighborhoods
- $3.6 million for illegal student loan servicing activity
- $100 million for creating new accounts not requested by customers to profit the bank
- $25 billion settlement for loan servicing and foreclosure fraud
- $50 million for overcharging homeowners for appraisals after foreclosure

There were others that Will was not able to read before security arrived. If only there was more time to expose the crimes of your kind's big banks against the peoples of the earth. They've been running roughshod over slaves, soldiers, migrants, natives, nations and ordinary hard-working people for centuries. Look no further in your research than the most profitable of business ventures: war. Of the banks, by the banks, for the banks is the hidden constitution of the oligarchs of your Western Civilization, if I can use the word "civilization" loosely.

You really should work harder and longer. Who else is going to pay the interest on the trillions of dollars of national blood and treasure debt they created if you aren't shackled to a miserable job and debt of your own? No need for chains when debt will do for the money masters of your kind. I know because I helped them do it, in the same way I've helped other predators take their prey. They are winning you know, in their march to own you and the world's resources, including the means of production and the means of destruction.

Which does explain why blaring through a bullhorn for a bank run would catch their attention. In terms of catching attention, only a few of your kind have mastered the activity better than Dowg. Thinking quickly, I convinced him to cut off the path of the security guards by placing himself between them and Will. Will's back was to the officers but the crowd was facing Dowg and the stairs, down which the guards were rapidly descending.

When the two Wells Fargo Security officers approached, Dowg turned his back to them, quickly pulled down his pants, bent over, and displayed his bare, white muscular ass to the approaching men in black.

With Dowg's full moon shining, the security pair slowed only slightly at the sight, fully expecting the usual verbiage to "Kiss my ass!" But Dowg said nothing between chuckles that were mounting into laughter. It's true, I convinced Dowg that the best way to run interference for Will was to take decisive action. I use the word "take" here somewhat loosely but mostly accurately, for in matters such as these, it's better to give than to receive.

With little time to waste, and giggling like a madman, Dowg squatted down, his naked buttocks hovering just above the marble steps. Relaxing slightly with a devilish grin, and a theatrical grunt, Dowg deposited an enormous mound of shit on the pristine imported stone of the bank's stairs. I've never really understood why some of you use the expression "take a shit" when in reality it's usually something that is left, dropped off, flushed, or in this case, deposited, or perhaps more accurately, invested.

I realize that most of your kind would find such indecent exposure, gifting or depositing to be unlawful, but for Dowg, it was a function of free speech only bettered by props that serve to reinforce deeper analogies. Similar to Dr. Spencer's ability to classify all sorts of flora and fauna into distinct categories, Dowg also put great effort into seeing things for what they are—and with equal importance—calling things by their proper names. In this case, any big bank that steals people's shit, treats people like shit, makes up shit, or any other such fraudulent and illegal bullshit—deserves some shit.

And once you are able to reason rightly by hearing me more clearly, you might be surprised at how good you get at calling shit by its proper name and putting it in the proper category of shit. What you do or do not do with this knowledge of properly named shit is still a conversation I always welcome. Dowg and I settled it years ago by determining when to take proper action in the face of properly-labeled shit, regardless of the consequences. Regardless of what they think of you and regardless of what they do to you.

As you might imagine, the security guards and officers of the law who apprehended Dowg that day did not appreciate that elusive form of beauty derived only from simplicity, from the natural. Even in the truth and beauty of the analogy of his deposit, it somehow escaped them when they issued a citation against him. They asked Dowg for his name and address, but without his wallet to demonstrate his ID, he gave them the name of the CEO of Wells Fargo.

Chapter 16 – Media Mouthpiece

While Dowg might occasionally use turds, Ben was more inclined to use words, especially in writing and speaking, for his initiation into *Hunt Club*. In line with the pursuit of his Masters of Fine Arts in Critical Media Studies at CU, Ben elected to present at the ***Digital and Social Media Conference*** in Vail, Colorado. Adept with the tool of language, Ben's presentation was to reveal the best methods for news outlets to conceal the truth from public consumers of mass media.

This test of the conference attendees would certainly include their ability to listen. For Dowg, it was a test of Ben's abilities to provide well-worded responses to insightful comments, or hopefully, inflammatory reactions from conference attendees. For Ben, it was about his family, his brother, and the big media and government lies perpetuated in the cover-up of his death. They called it friendly fire. It was so warm and friendly in fact, that the friend shot him at point blank range three times through the forehead. Yes, it's true, I convinced Ben's brother Pat that the U.S. invasion of Afghanistan had nothing to do with smoking boogeymen out of their hidey-holes in the hills. He began to question the purpose of the war. And like most good questions posed by thinking types, your empire answers them all the same way: with bullets.

When they merged onto Interstate 70 towards Vail, Dowg noted the unending stream of Subaru's, semis, SUVs, and Humvees; trucks and tourists locked in a race to overheat their engines on the uphills and melt their brake rotors on the downhills. Nothing like a distracted tourist taking a high mountain interstate corner at 85 mph Dowg thought to himself, not to mention the distracted drivers on their devices. "Gawd damn texters," Dowg muttered out loud, "they're going to get us all killed with their pathetic addiction to meaningless conversations and childish amusements."

Watching Ben's grip on the wheel vary from fairly firm to death grasp, in sync with fully justified bouts of fear and rage, Dowg devised a simple plan. Any speeding or distracted driver was offered the chance to view his bare buttocks pressed firmly against the passenger window for the violator to plainly see, point out, comment on, and photograph as Colorado wildlife if so inclined.

Coasting and braking into Vail, they arrived in time to create a meal out of the conference finger food before they hustled to the assigned presentation room. Dowg, who had

chosen to borrow Will's Goodwill suit from the Wells
Fargo prank, fit rather inconspicuously among the
attendees, despite the many dog hairs clinging to his pants
and lapels. Near the door stood an easel bearing the
presentation's titles and times, including Ben's:

*Dis-Misinformation Identification, Creation &
Dissemination: Best Practices for the Digital Age.*

*Ben A. Blair, ADHDPHD, PTSDMD, RNADNA, MADD,
DUDE*

*Center for Information Analysis and Response, Federal
Communications Commission.*

Ben strolled to the computer projecting onto a large screen
at the front of the room while Dowg stood in the back,
scanning and counting nearly 50 attendees. Mostly media
specialists from various news outlets, some from larger
conglomerates and corporate news whose symbols Dowg
recognized on their names tags tucked into the plastic
badges hanging from their necks.

Yes, it's true, Ben chugged half a bottle water to wash
down his cottonmouth before launching into his
presentation on how to best deceive consumers of mass
media news. He explained the utility and applicability of

his research for large organizations, especially corporations and nation states. Dowg watched Ben intently for any signs of embarrassment or fear as he presented a brief history of "public relations" and its purposes.

Beginning with Sigmund Freud's nephew, Edward Bernays and concluding with Noam Chomsky, Ben explained how "public relations" and "propaganda" can effectively shape public opinion, whether it be to promote cigarette smoking among women or to manufacture consent for the nation-state to wage illegal wars for empire. Perceptions must be managed and manipulated in the same way the truth must be diminished, dismembered, disparaged and concealed.

Having committed his work to memory, Ben pressed on with the presentation of the following slides:

Dis-Misinformation Identification, Creation & Dissemination: Best Practices for the Digital Age

The results of this analysis revealed trends and patterns in public relations and consent manufacturing that provide useful insights for organizations of all sizes, in both public and private sectors. Depending on your agenda and the undue influence of special interests on your organization, presented here are three components of an effective sequence worthy of your expert consideration:

1. Identification

• This analysis has demonstrated that the number one way to identify misinformation about your organization is to focus on those using demonstrable and accurate facts to tell the truth. This would likely include ethical employees or citizens, whistleblowers and fact-centric reporters and researchers.

• Content and image analysis of news and audio clips and photographs revealed that in any society, the mothers are primary sources of misinformation. In certain circumstances, they can be far more effective in reaching audiences with their message than your organizations and thus they should be avoided. These might include:

    - Middle Eastern mothers grieving the losses of their homes and families vaporized by US, British, French, and Russian bombs.

    - US, British, French and Russian mothers who have lost their sons and daughters, because they were sent to vaporize the Middle East with bombs of democracy, liberty, and pursuit of happiness missiles.

    - Palestinian mothers grieving the bullet-ridden bodies of their sons and daughters who were gunned down for throwing rocks at bulldozers levelling their humble homes and olive orchards.

- Latin American mothers watching their families suffer, starve and die as a direct result of hegemonic US policy, election meddling and drug smuggling in their own countries.

- American Mothers watching their sons and daughters, husbands and friends succumb from a life of addiction to legalized pharmaceutical opioids.

- African Mothers watching their sons and daughters suffer, starve and then die from malnourishment, artificially-created diseases and plundering warlords.

- Asian mothers watching themselves and their offspring live short hard lives of poverty and misery as disposable slaves enduring long days of monotonous labor in corporate sweatshops.

Ben momentarily paused for effect and surveyed the faces before him. Some seemed confused, others appeared to be unsure, but the bulk of attendees were caught in that wasteland of thought between the borders of poor listening and a brain distracted by an electronic device.

Identification Best Practices

• Once you have identified the sources of truthful information being disseminated to the public and damaging the public's perception of your organization, it is recommended that organizations:

1. Repudiate the truthful information as soon as possible even if there is no rational basis for your claim that the truthful information is false. Think vigorous sell, not fact checking. Coordinate with larger media organizations such as Facebook and YouTube to have the information censored and removed.

2. Develop and apply useful words or expressions to label and thus categorize the truthful information to maximize repudiation effects. Select expressions might include: "could not be confirmed," "untrue," "fake news," "regime propaganda," "false reports," "alleged," or "they claim" with mockery.

3. Conduct a public assassination of the character of the individual(s) who disseminated the truthful information. Research their pasts and find any useful video, postings or individuals with information that could be crafted to fit your purposes. Be creative in undermining their credibility and the truth.

4. Repeat steps 1-3 for all cases involving truth tellers. These are likely to include rigorous journalists or documentary film makers who

reported on facts that are not the sort of facts you would report. Simply repeat steps 1-3.

2. Creation

• After identifying, labeling and repudiating misinformation, and upon successful completion of the character assassination, be sure to take the necessary time for thoughtful consideration to create some information of your own.

• Be creative, and if possible, avoid being critical in the early stages of brainstorming. Criticism at this stage may affect group morale, creativity and sensitivity for the facts.

• Be open to seemingly unbelievable ideas and exaggerations. Avoid putting your mind into a box to think outside of. Be as clever and as imaginative as possible.

Ben scanned the faces of the audience and was delighted to see several of them smiling. Some still appeared to be confused but listening while others exhibited twisted frowns, squinted and shook their heads from side to side.

Creation Best Practices

• The current analysis reveals that the best method for creating information is to have no source from which the information came. Despite your creative brainstorming, avoid taking credit for the working ideas. The following actions are recommended:

1. Establish that a person, whether in a government, corporate or secretive institution, would be willing to confirm, or augment, your newly created information. If successful, the most useful expression to apply is "officials have revealed" without revealing the officials.

2. If you are unable to establish an official to confirm or augment your imaginative figments, don't worry—simply create one!

   a. Remember, it's a face that you need, not the facts. It is recommended that your organization pursues a wealthy, sharply-dressed white male, in his fifties or older. It is important to assure that your man posing as an official expert exudes more confidence than care for the truth.

   b. Ideally, your newly-created official hasn't appeared in the news and press enough for anyone to conduct thorough background research on his credentials, connections and accomplishments.

3. Regardless of the confirmation of your information by officials and non-officials, useful expressions to overcome this minor concern in

information creation include "sources that cannot be revealed have told us," "witnesses have said," and "our sources have found."

3. Dissemination:

• Whether confirmed or unconfirmed, once you have created your information, consider the ABCD's of these high-impact best practices to disseminate your creative works for maximum effect:

1. *Act Quickly*: Possess a sense of urgency, especially when disseminating flammable information intended to disparage truth tellers who may counter your agenda. It is recommended that you do not waste time with such matters as researching or confirming any facts. The attention span of your average viewer is far too short. It is important to counter them before they've made up their minds and moved on.

2. *Be Continuous*: Your creativity does not end with the development of your newly fashioned information. More is needed using various non-existent sources to leak the information using the most effective channels so as not to jeopardize any misperceptions of your organization. A best practice is to advantage your organization by also

173

questioning the validity of the information you created so as to appear neutral or even skeptical.

3. *Correction Minimization*: Publish your created information no less than three times in multiple news outlets. Only after your creative work has been fully refuted, should you issue any kind of a correction. If you must issue a correction, do so in very fine print in an inconspicuous place near the end of any written or video broadcast pieces. It is not a best practice to issue any retractions of your creative and imaginative work.

4. *Dismiss*: It will advantage your organization to dismiss tellers and triangulators of truthful information by publishing misleading or altered pictures or video taken out of context. Whenever possible, dismiss thinking people and their difficult questions to better manage their perceptions and to manufacture consent for your agenda.

"Thank you for your time and attention today. I appreciate this opportunity," Ben concluded.

"Any questions?"

Ben and Dowg scanned the room for any raised hands or questioning looks among the attendees. Some were still busy poking at their electronic devices with fingers and thumbs while others frowned, nodded, or furrowed their brows in perplexity. The silence was deafening, especially to Dowg, who was increasingly disappointed by the lack of questions. Shifting nervously in his seat, waiting impatiently for audience participation, Dowg slowly and deliberately began to raise his hand, when he was overruled by a loud voice.

In the back of the room near the door stood a large man with a stern face, his thick neck laced with badges and credentials that came to rest at the top of his asymmetrically large belly.

"This man is a fraud! He doesn't work for the Center for Information Analysis and Response!"

There was a murmur from the crowd as they turned their heads to see the accuser. This was followed by another murmur when they swiveled their heads back to stare at Ben as if it were a grand-slam tennis match.

Dowg calmed down and sat back in his chair, eager to watch Ben handle the accusation. Content that Ben was on the spot, Dowg watched his face closely for any sign of flushing, fear or embarrassment.

"Show us your ID," the stern man boomed, making his way toward Ben, who clearly was racking his brain for some sort of a reasonable response.

"I need to see *your* ID," Ben retorted, feigning offense that he had been called a fraud.

The crowd was audibly confused, and Dowg chuckled, watching Ben do his best to fend off the surly man using an assortment of words that didn't convince him or the conference officials who had arrived to quell the unrest. Dowg's chuckles grew into laughter and howling after Ben audaciously asked the officials and arriving officers to show him *two* forms of ID. Dowg's howling caught their attention, and they turned their heads to look at him. On my command, Dowg took decisive action.

"Wanna see *my* ID?" Dowg asked loudly, jumping atop the two nearest chairs. Balancing himself, Dowg unzipped the dark blue pants of his borrowed suit.

"I like to call this my *corporate media mouthpiece!*" he crowed before reaching into his pants to display an object to the conference attendees. There was no mistaking that what he had taken out of his pants was not, in fact, a microphone.

Yes, it's true, Dowg held his long, limp pecker firmly at its base with his hand and waved it gleefully for all attendees to see.

For such a lean man, Dowg was remarkably well-endowed. Some people stared in amazement; others turned away in disgust, still others recorded the spectacle with their devices. Dowg quickly scanned the faces of the media moguls and peons until he settled on the confused face of one woman who stood aghast at his display, her mouth wide open. She wore expensive clothes, a tidy hairdo, thick makeup, and was adorned with several colorful badges covered in corporate logos. Perfect, he thought to himself.

"Would you like some of this while I got it out?" Dowg asked the appalled woman, brandishing his flaccid manhood and hairy scrotum at her. These were to be Dowg's last words of the conference before he ended up at the bottom of another fun scrum pile of security officers.

Yes, like Will, Ben also escaped unharmed. For Dowg, it's like raising a puppy—he would never let a young one stray too far off leash in such a dangerous jungle infested with so many big corporate cats.

Chapter 17 – The Smiling Valve Turner

Are words more powerful than wrenches? It's a good question, and I've discussed it much with the action-oriented types of your kind for years, spanning generations and nation-states. For those less inclined to use words, the wrench ascends to its rightful place as the proper tool for change, especially for Aldo. I convinced him that words would have no real effect on Anadarko Petroleum, their fracking wells, waste, tanks, and pipelines or even on fracking politicians suffering from that toxic mental illness of greed.

Your kind has developed a strange relationship with your very own mother earth that could be easily described as abusive and perverted. Instead of thanking and respecting her for her beauty and generosity, you seem bent on devising the most effective methods to rape and pillage her. Every which way of course, horizontally and vertically, because looser is better for these motherfrackers. They'll drill her anywhere, from the warm and gentle waters of the Gulf of Mexico to the frigid ice of the North Pole to the sunny domains of your national parks and public lands. These frackers go deep, go long, go strong and when they've reached her profit-laden core with their rods of steel, they spew in her their toxic chemical loads of poisonous carcinogenic goo.

These very same motherfrackers will also tell you that the fouling of your air and water and the rumbling earthquakes of your deeply-drilled mother are unrelated to their abusive perversions. Aldo knew this to be true from both experience and from doing his reading, even of letters to his father from the motherfrackers who'd fouled their farm's water, air and worth. Aldo and I have conversed more than once on this topic of fracking one's own mother, and it was in a recent discussion that we devised a reasonable course of action. Or what I sometimes call an actionable course of reason in my line of work.

The plan was not complex, and with Dowg's consent, Aldo chose to exact it at night. Halsey would be the witness, and for this test, he would also be the lookout. Will drove the truck and came to a complete stop at the intersection of County Roads 60 and 15, well beyond the outskirts of Windsor, Colorado. Aldo and Halsey glided out of the back of the truck unnoticed in the night's darkness. They remained motionless, lying flat in the shallow impression of the roadside ditch, watching the headlights of the truck fade from sight.

They scurried from the ditch into a farmer's field with their gear, deeper into the blackness, further from the illuminating headlights of any passing vehicles. Moving quickly, quietly and low-to-the-ground, they covered the distance across the field to an irrigation ditch adjoining the two farmlands on which they were trespassing. Opposite them stood the liquids separation tanks and supporting pipes, valves and levers neatly encaged in fencing surrounded by a berm of gravel banking.

Concealed in the darkness of the ditch, they quietly readied their gear. From his pack, Halsey pulled out a black, Monte Carlo buttstock and began assembling a very expensive and reliable Walther pellet gun with a night-vision scope and silencer.

Aldo pulled from his pack a neatly-fitting monkey mask, complete with a permanent grin, hairy head and sideburns that connected at the chin to make the beard but no mustache. He fit the mask over his face followed by the head straps of a pair of night vision goggles courtesy of Halsey. Then Aldo produced from his pack a Heckler and Koch Co2 BB pistol, which he quickly slipped into the right back pocket of his field tan pants. Yes, it's true, they had agreed that no firearms would be used but that air guns were permissible and less susceptible to ballistics testing.

Last from his pack, Aldo grasped 18 inches of bolt cutters in his left hand and another 18 inches of rapid-grip pipe wrench in his right hand.

"Are we in it to win it?" Halsey whispered. Having completed the assembly of his air rifle and affixed it to its bipod, he peered through the night-vision scope to scan the fenced-in facility that housed their tall hardened metallic enemies.

Aldo nodded, his monkey mask grinning eerily in the dark. He took a deep breath and moved forward up the ditch, careful to stay low. Reaching the southwest corner of the facility's perimeter, he lay flat on the bank of the ditch to better see the battery of steely foes and Halsey aiming at them.

Aldo could hear the muffled bursts of air from Halsey's rifle and the swift zips of the lead pellets through the still night air. Each shot was systematically and rhythmically timed for maximum efficiency and effectiveness. Aldo could see the three cameras atop slender steel rods twitch and jolt with every penetration of a projectile. Occasionally he heard the sound of the tinkle of breaking and falling glass between the varying high-pitched hums of lead ricocheting off steel.

Halsey emptied his first clip on the surveillance cameras, quickly reloaded, and rhythmically shot through the control panels and electrical instruments tied to their corresponding solar charged batteries. On his third clip, Halsey shot the four visible solar panels that powered the electrical needs of the facility's instruments.

Content with having softened the surveillance battlefield, Halsey waved to Aldo to advance in the next phase of their actionable course of reason. Halsey watched through his night-vision scope as the smiling monkey scrambled quickly out of the ditch and ran rapidly toward the fence. The image of a sprinting, grinning and well-purposed primate, with pipe wrench and bolt cutters in hands, and a pistol butt protruding from his back pocket—all these struck Halsey as perfectly congruent, the natural stuff of anthropoids and their evolutions.

Even more congruent, thought Halsey as he watched Aldo withdraw his pistol and shoot four BBs into a security camera lurking behind the easternmost tank, outside of Halsey's sniping view. Working swiftly, he threw the pipe wrench and bolt cutters over the chain link barrier and quickly scaled it to land in the maze of tanks and pipes, gauges and valves.

Three simple criteria guided the strategy: if a valve is on, turn it off, starting with the mains. If a valve is off, turn it on. If a device runs on electricity, disable it. Moving quickly, Aldo went to the main gas line, cut the chain holding the valve and spun it shut. He speedily applied the adjustable pipe wrench to the square bolts of the valve turns, beginning with the largest pipes.

Halsey watched through the scope as the grinning monkey worked speedily, turning on, but mostly turning off, valves big and then small. Advancing next to electricity, Aldo stepped toward the solar power main box and firmly swung the pipe wrench through it, shattering the glass and breaking the electrical components. He was drawing back to administer another stroke of the wrench when he was arrested by the sight of headlights appearing on the gravel country road.

His heart pounding, Aldo slipped behind a holding tank and lay flat on his stomach as the vehicle slowed, turned towards the facility, and came to a stop. Halsey watched patiently through his scope. A man stepped out of the truck and walked around the front of it to the passenger side.

Listening intently without showing himself, Aldo tried to gauge the man's proximity by the sound of his footsteps on the gravel.

Straining to hear over the idling truck engine, Aldo heard what plainly sounded like a heavy-duty fart. He inched closer to the side of the holding tank, and with his night vision goggles was able to see the stranger releasing a long, warm stream of urine onto the gravel pullout. Upon completing his bodily function, and emitting one more loud, reverberating fart, the man hopped back into his truck and drove off. Aldo let out his breath and as the headlights faded into the night, he sprang up with his tools, ran to the fence, and threw the bolt cutters over. Turning around and wielding the 18 inch pipe wrench in his right hand, the still smiling monkey disabled the two remaining solar panels with mighty blows of the wrench.

Halsey watched Aldo sprint back toward the fence and ascend it by pushing off the chain links with his feet. Reaching the zenith of his running climb, he firmly grabbed the top of the fence with the pipe wrench before scrambling over to land on his feet. Adjusting his night vision goggles, the permanently grinning primate stooped to grab the bolt cutters before he escaped into the petroleum jungle that is Colorado's Front Range.

Chapter 18 – WNS - October

You've probably considered the importance of a good metal tool or twelve in your life. I've said it before; metal has shaped the empires and tools of your kind for centuries with all sorts of harmful and healthful outcomes. Deciding on the proper tool for the job is a conversation I've had with many other species long before you arrived. Long before your rulers put you on the path to slave labor to procure evermore enormously expensive metal tools meant only to maximize killing.

You really ought to be for more strict gun, bomb and missile restrictions; your governments kill people by the millions with these highly-refined tools of destruction. Mass shootings and bombings on a near daily basis are committed by the West's war machine, yet there is no talk of bomb control, let alone self-control among your war-mongering politicians and misled masses. By a few strokes of their pens, they unleash their metallic tools of death to terrorize, maim, kill, and char the flesh of any life form that gets in the way of their profits.

For Houndman, this was no way to smoke a chicken, and for Anthony, no way to treat vegetables, especially at *Wednesday Night Services*. When Will arrived at the Glen

Haven Inn, he was met with the usual aromas of smoked and grilled foods followed by the sounds of conversation, laughter and Metro's guitar starting into a Jack Johnson cover. Topping the stairs, he saw tall, stone-faced Zeno in conversation with Anthony, who was rotating onions on the grill.

As Will came upon Dr. Schwede, who was as usual working on his tablet at the nearest table on the deck, the revered professor of engineering looked up to greet Will and inquire about progress on his project.

Will glanced about them to assure that no one was listening. "I revisited the code you created for the defense system software devised to penetrate the control systems of ships," Will replied, tone hushed.

Dr. Schwede broke into a smile, and his face lit up brightly before he glanced around the deck himself.

"And?"

"I augmented the guidance control software to not only disable a vehicle but have it recommunicate with GPS satellites and systems, which will allow the vehicle to be remotely controlled in simulations. With access to military grade GPS systems, it is possible that a vehicle can be penetrated and remotely controlled at a distance using a tablet if the software code was…"

They were interrupted first by Old Cassee barking loudly, followed by a loud gasp from Metro, who had suddenly stopped playing his guitar. Attendees looked up to see the figure of a large man scaling the deck's mountainside railing. After he landed neatly on the deck, the man, as hairy as he was filthy, wild-eyed as he was forlorn, stood and looked at everyone. After a short but seemingly long and awkward silence, the man, who seemed to magically appear from the woods, simply began to cry.

I've pointed H.L. Michaelsen, or Cletus for those that know him, out before. You can see him in the picture at the bottom, just to the left of center, with his head propped on his elbow on a stone table.

"Is that you Cletus?" Samuel asked with some surprise and concern as Houndman tried to quiet Cassee's barking.

"This certainly has changed since I was here last," Cletus wept to no one in particular.

Looking him over, Dr. Spencer noticed that his scratched and filthy legs and feet appeared to be swollen from accumulating and retaining fluid. Flesh was beginning to bulge out against his torn, tattered and worn-out moccasins. "Edema," he thought to himself, taking a closer look at Cletus's feet.

"What have you been doing with yourself these days Cletus?" Samuel asked, smiling at the unexpected visitor who'd dropped in from the Crosier Mountain side of the Inn.

"I decided to leave society and live in the Wilderness," he replied between sniffles, "I've had my fill of humans and opted instead for more solitude."

"What you have been eating?" Anthony asked with demonstrable concern for the filthy, malnourished wilderness wanderer.

"Grass, berries, dandelions, blue flax seeds and mushrooms, mainly," Cletus replied, wiping his moist eyes to better see what was cooking on the grill and smoker.

Will looked at Aldo, who looked at Ben. Ben shrugged and opened his palms. They enjoyed the variation in surprises at WNS and did consider that they had never really attended the same service twice.

When Dowg arrived from his walkabout with Pearly and Jack on Glen Haven's trails, the dogs greeted all WNS attendees with equality of enthusiasm and affection save for one: Broad. You might think that I am the one who told you to trust your gut for sound judgement—not always true, you'll do far better to trust me and your dog than your gut, especially if you don't eat right.

Broad made his way to the grill area to converse with Houndman, who was overseeing the smoker, soaking more wood chips and turning chicken breasts.

"Broad, just wanted to let you know that I'm conducting a reading in *Weekly Seminar* next week and hope that you'll be there," Houndman offered.

"And what will you be reading?" Broad asked.

"I'm reading an article that I wrote on probability logic. It addresses the impossibility of artificially created contradictions," Houndman replied.

"How can you write on this topic when your argument refutes itself?" Broad replied. His voice squeaked annoyingly.

Ol' Cassee, who had been lying next to Houndman, and Pearly, who was sitting next to Dowg, felt their Alpha's energies change from pleasant to plainly perturbed. Both dogs looked Broad directly in the eyes and uttered very low, nearly inaudible growls.

"Behold the perfect circle!" Dowg barked loudly.

"A perfect circle?"

"Isn't that the official form for a conceited anal sphincter?" Dowg asked.

"Or are we dealing with a square here?" he added sarcastically, stroking his chin for effect as if it would help him arrive at the correct answer.

Anthony glanced their way and shot them a frown of disapproval. It was the same frown he reserved for attendees who were talking about politicians or gawd fear.

"I'll get that little prick," Houndman whispered with a smile to his hound Ol' Cassee. "You know it is a royal privilege to do good and be ill-spoken of," he murmured with a wry grin as he massaged the dog's neck.

They sat down for their meal in the cool of the October evening and the bantering Broad of CU took up conversation with CSU's Dr. Spencer.

"Have you had a chance to read my rejoinder on income inequality in the *American Journal of International Law*?" Broad asked.

"Was that your rejoinder?" Houndman interjected before Spencer could answer. "That I built a fire with yesterday morning?" he added with a palpable sense of thankfulness for the warmth it had provided his cabin.

Ignoring him, Broad instead turned to Spencer for his reply.

"I believe their criticisms of your construct are valid, especially in relation to your explanations for income equality involving work and money," Spencer suggested. "Your position for controls on population size and on wealth are contrary to living one's life in accordance with natural laws. Furthermore, your position that money should only be allowed for commerce and not accumulation is complicated more by your position that interest-bearing loans should be forbidden under threat of punishment."

"To solve the inequality problem, we would agree that the concept of money must be addressed. As we see in your model, Spencer," Broad stated, "the rich become richer, and the divide between the haves and have-nots keeps widening with each corrupt marble hall buyoff of the democratically elected. The happiness of the citizens of the state cannot depend on wealth and power. Rather, the state should promote virtue and social harmony, both of which are undermined by economic inequality. Thus, I maintain my position that the ignorant masses—who should be termed *The Beast*, should be frugal and their money should be controlled. Ideally, cash money should be banned in favor of digital currencies that can be monitored," he concluded authoritatively.

Dowg shook his head and smirked. "Broad, despite your annoying and hypocritical virtue signaling, what makes you think that you're smart enough to micromanage everyone's life?"

Before Broad could reply, Spencer broke in. "While I agree that many men have confused the proper use of money with the possession and accumulation of it, men should be free to barter and exchange as they please with a currency also of their choosing. There is no need for the state to control the wealth of the citizens. But it is sensible that the wealth obtained by the state should be used *for* the citizens. It is as natural to acquire wealth as it is to have tremendous variation in work skills and knowledge among the people. I still maintain that liberty among citizens and the just application of the rule of law will most contribute to their happiness."

"Well put Spencer," Dowg stated emphatically. "I would add that self-rule most contributes to happiness among virtuous people. Broad clearly advocates running all of our lives, probably with some special counsel or an elite state club or bureau composed of equally conceited peckerheads. Which begs the obvious question to you, Broad—what will prevent your beloved club of elitist pricks from being bought off and swayed with bribes and blackmail when they take their turns bent over a lobbyist's pickle barrel?"

Broad paused momentarily before answering. "They will be specially trained and educated by the state," he responded softly.

Dowg's howls of laughter filled the mountain air and echoed from the Inn's deck and walls off the Crosier Mountain side. Other attendees looked to see him slapping his knee and rocking forward and backwards in his chair until he wiped his watering eyes. "Specially trained?" Dowg yelped. "On how to run other people's lives? Oh wise king?!" he followed sarcastically, grinning and shaking his head from side to side.

"I see nothing but smoke in your elitist club, Broad," Dowg continued. "All around those dollar signs in their beady eyes when they scamper through the sewers with their bribes like rats. Your club is even more corruptible more quickly than the "democratically" elected club in Spencer's model. Either way, we end up with another pretentious Ivy League "educated" trust-fund brat leading the shitshow. Not because they are leaders, but because they rode daddy's coattails to power, meandering along some corporate path guarded by similarly-minded, jive-ass frat boy types." He smirked. "It's nothing but smoke."

Houndman grinned and looked up to see Cletus half-listening to the discussion. His head was propped up by his arm and elbow on the table, (just as we see him in the picture), and he brimmed with melancholy, softly weeping in despair for his own kind and his disdain for them.

"Are you a mercenary?" Aldo inquired of Halsey several ales later.

Samuel shot Halsey a quick glance before returning his gaze to Houndman, who was intent on finding another copy of Broad's manuscript so that he could start a fire in the chiminea.

"Something like that," Halsey replied. "I'm not in the regular army anymore, but suffice it to say that I still work with the Pentagon as a defense contractor for a security company called *Academi*."

"Had enough of the army?" Will asked.

"You could say that," Halsey replied, pondering a suitable answer to the question.

Yes, it's true, Halsey was discharged from the US Army Green Berets for severely beating an Afghan police commander aligned with US forces in Afghanistan.

"You know it's common practice for some Afghan men to have these dancing boys that they dress up as little girls and then bang the hell out of them," he said. "I've heard it with my own ears and seen them with my own eyes. The Afghan commander working with our unit had kidnapped a little boy from his mother, a local village woman, chained him to a bed, and assaulted him for a week. Then he assaulted the boy's mother when she begged for the little guy back. Eventually the mother came to us for help, so my captain and I arranged a meeting with the Afghani commander."

"What happened next?" Ben asked impatiently.

"He admitted to raping the boy but laughed at our concern for the harm to the child and his family, which my Captain didn't take very well. He took it about as well as the Afghani commander took the Captain's first, well-placed punch to his face. While he was on the ground but still conscious and fighting back, I jumped on top of that Afghan boy banger and beat every trace of laughter out of him," Halsey replied with only minimal satisfaction but no regret.

"It was a great way to piss off the generals," Halsey explained. "Even more so when I made clear my refusal to work anymore with US *allies* in the Middle East," he added with a twisted smile. "You probably know that the US government arms and funds terrorists in the Middle East," Halsey continued after glancing casually around him. "Despite the efforts of a handful of congressmen, and one good-looking Hawaiian congresswoman, they couldn't get a bill passed to end US support of terrorists. Since I refused to work with these terrorists, the army claimed that I had switched sides in the pipeline wars, but rather than court-martial me, I was discharged," he explained with little emotion and maximum indifference.

After a brief pause, Halsey spun the top off his shiny silver whiskey flask and took a generous two-tug pull chased by another two-tug pull of beer.

The fire in the chiminea had burned down to tiny red coals when Halsey was awakened by the fierce need to urinate.

3:14 AM

He eased his half-drunk and fully naked body out of his warm sleeping bag under the stars, put on his boots and made his way down the steps of the Inn towards the parking lot along the road. Peering into the darkness, he only half-listened to the stream of beer and whiskey urine meandering its way to the road's edge.

The cool morning mountain air sharpened Halsey's groggy mind enough to hear the offbeat intermittent sounds of clanging metal. Turning, he looked in the direction of the Glen Haven General Store, just down from the Inn, and across the narrow road. Halsey focused his eyes on the building and noted the motion detection light was activated to illuminate a large bear sniffing and testing the bear-proof dumpster.

"Black Bear!" his foggy brain told him as his little river of piss came to a trickling end.

Very quietly, Halsey slipped in and out of the vehicles and opened the door of his truck. He rummaged through the ever-present black duffle until he found the proper metallic tool. Naked with the exception of his boots, Halsey stood by his truck brandishing a state-of-the-art paintball gun fully loaded with bright pink orbs.

Halsey assured that the CO_2 canister was twisted tight to the gun and quickly slipped unnoticed across the road, careful to avoid the pale glow of the lone street light. The bear punched and pulled at the dumpster lid; unaware of the nearing naked human, it stayed focused on the food and the frustration of the uncooperative contraption. Halsey crept to the rear of the general store and peered around the building's corner to see the large animal fully engrossed in its problem-solving, using powerful strokes of its paws.

Halsey raised the gun and shot repeatedly at the dark furry mass of the bear's hind end. The sounds of the paintballs exploding against the metal dumpster and the sting of the paintballs on the bear's thick fur was enough to scare it into immediate flight. Unsure of the source and direction from which the exploding balls came, the bear swiftly scrambled around the front of the general store in the direction of the sleeping inn and neighboring town hall.

Will sat up groggily in his sleeping bag, awakened by the commotion and sound of the assault on the metal dumpster by bear and paintballs. Listening intently, he tried to make sense of the sound of running footsteps that seemed to be coming closer to him. Will squinted towards the lone street light to see a large brown black bear sprinting in full strides along the road's shoulder. Will rubbed his eyes to see that the bear sported bright pink blotches on its midsection, back and hindquarters.

Will then heard the soft bursts of CO_2 and the whizzing and bursting paintballs followed by more running feet. He looked again toward the streetlight to see the lily-white butt cheeks of a naked human pursuing the slightly faster bear. Passing from under the glow of the street light, the sprinters disappeared over the dirt and down the sandy bank of West Creek.

Will heard the bear run through the creek, but he could not see the splattering paintballs annoying the bear to higher ground on the other side of the creek. After reaching a higher and safer point, the bear stopped momentarily to look back and huff loudly at the human for the unwelcome hazing.

Will glanced at the empty sleeping bag on the deck and made the connection that the furless cheeks of the long-legged human sprinter belonged to Halsey. He reappeared from the creek bottom and strolled casually down and across Hwy 43 towards the inn.

Yes, it's true, Halsey was well-known for his endurance and marksmanship on and off the battlefield. Just as well-known as I am to recommend never chasing a bear butt naked with only your boots on.

Chapter 19 - Smooth Skinned

Our list of worthwhile tools has grown from axes and wrenches to splitting mauls and bolt cutters to paintball guns. By default, our list must include knives. Even the bread knife Houndman set down before putting two slices of fresh lentil bread into the toaster. It was a cool October Saturday morning, and Will took another sip of coffee and continued salivating with Dowg and the dogs over the smell of bacon and frying eggs.

Will knew to eat well—there was another planned workout with wood at the *Swift Dog Gym.* The dogs were temporarily distracted from the food by the arrival of Samuel entering the sliding glass door. Their tails wagged and their jealousy was made plain by their playful competition for Samuel's affections.

"That quarrelsome wife of yours again?" Houndman asked with a wink and a grin before he poured a cup of coffee for his mentor of old.

Samuel simply smiled and sat down with Dowg and Will at the table.

"Any advice to a young man thinking about marriage or not?" Houndman asked.

"Whatever he does, he will regret it," Samuel stated with supreme confidence, "but by all means marry—if you get a good wife, you'll become happy—if you get a bad one, you'll become a philosopher."

"But be careful," Houndman cautioned, "if she's beautiful, you'll never have her for yourself, and if she is ugly, you'll pay for it dearly."

"The reality is," Dowg interjected, "if you are young, put marriage off for a while. If you are old, it's probably too late."

"Women are unavoidable stress you know," Dowg added, "They are the source of much deception and misery for men."

"But what of the wise women out there?" Houndman retorted. "Virtue is the same for women as for men."

"Not in that order or in the same proportions," Dowg muttered in response. "After all, what has a woman ever done that a man didn't do before her?"

"Wise men know who is worthy to be loved, and they will not refrain from loving or making love to beautiful women who appreciate a virtuous man," Houndman countered.

"Lovers derive their pleasures from their misfortunes and co-dependence," Dowg replied. "An open union between a man who persuades, and a woman who consents, is a far superior relationship than marriage and all the myths and traditions surrounding it. Mathematically, who could possibly trust an institution of our society that fails approximately 50% of the time? Wouldn't that be a one-in-two chance the next dumb sucker to marry will have to split up his life, children, friends and wealth?"

Houndman altered the subject of splitting slightly by turning Will's attention to the firewood and how it would be arranged. In the center of the bark-covered *Swift Dog Gym* floor, Will and Houndman had stacked stones to create a large fire pit. With the firepit as the center point, the split firewood was loosely piled into two long semicircles with a radius of approximately 25 paces from the stone pit. Little remained of the original stack of logs. They had been reduced to firewood by Will's fall labors, enhanced by increasingly efficient, accurate and stronger swings of the splitting maul.

Houndman listened to the telltale sounds of well-placed swings and splitting wood while he readied two smaller pine logs, both approximately seven feet long and eight inches in diameter. Propping one of them onto the unsplit rounds, Houndman sat and straddled the log where he sharpened the long slender blade of a draw knife using a file.

"Skinning logs is a lot like a relationship with a good woman," Houndman stated, testing the knife's sharpness with his thumb. "It's both a form of art and form of work to achieve a work of art," he added before grasping the curvy smooth wooden handles of the steel blade.

"First, be gentle. If it requires too much effort, consider a more seasoned piece. No need to test your patience on something green, you'll likely scar it up unnecessarily," Houndman began.

"Second, go with the grain. Top down, or from the bottom up, nothing else will do," he clarified before effortlessly peeling a long strip of dead bark and cambium to a knot in the log.

"Third, don't wear yourself or dull your blade on a tough knot; you'll likely scar it up even worse." Setting the draw knife down, Houndman grabbed a sharp hatchet firmly in his right hand.

"Solve the tough knot problems by going with the grain using firm accuracy," Houndman explained before swiftly swinging the hatchet. Will heard the loud ping of the stroke of the metal head and saw the severed knot skip once on the ground before it ricocheted off a bigger piece of wood.

Taking his turn, Will picked up the drawknife and straddled the log. Gently drawing the blade toward himself, he skinned the bark and cambium of the Ponderosa Pine into long strips that fell neatly curled at his feet. As the aromatic scent of pine filled the air, Will settled into smooth long strokes of the blade that had a calming, therapeutic effect on him.

"It's about bringing out the natural beauty," Houndman indicated, running his rough hands over the smooth curves of the white flesh of the wood, "which unlike artificial beauty, cannot be improved upon, you know."

"What will this be used for?" Will asked.

"It's going to be wine rack for a lady friend," Houndman said with a wink, a wide grin and thoughtful eyes. "Mmmm Mmmm—now that's a good woman," Houndman confessed, half smacking his lips as if he were consuming a rare and delightful food.

"And the other log to be skinned?" Will inquired smiling.

"That's for the pack to enjoy," Houndman answered with an even wider smile, but he did not elaborate any more on what that exactly meant.

Chapter 20 - Hunting with Dowg - November

Yes, it's true, some of the best small-game rodent hunting can be found on a university campus. Not to be confused with university administrators, the rodents abounding on campuses are best distinguished by their minimal fear of humans and even some dogs. You may have encountered some of these assertive tree rodents at your institution or alma mater, easily noted by their obesity, twitchy tails and beady, shifty eyes.

With a little time before the start of *Weekly Seminar* at CU's campus, Dowg thought it best to use it wisely and drop in on Professor Broad's class. He slipped in quietly with two other students and found a seat in the back of the class just as Broad was beginning the day's lecture.

"Good morning class," Broad said in his weak, almost inaudible voice, "we'll begin today reading from our assigned articles on metaphysics, specifically, the sun as a metaphor of the form of the good."

Dowg looked about the classroom at the students, most of whom were retrieving the article from their devices, a few from their book bags.

"Any idea what he is talking about?" Dowg whispered to the graduate student to his left. "What is the form of the good?"

The student did not engage Dowg at his question, aside from a quick glance at the homeless man before turning back to his device. Without looking up, Broad moved on to the second paragraph of the article in his monotone reading voice.

Seizing the moment, Dowg pulled a small, flat package wrapped in tin foil from his coat pocket. The graduate student on Dowg's right glanced over to see him opening the foil to reveal a salmon fillet that had been recently alder-smoked by Houndman.

"Would you like to try some?" Dowg invitingly asked the student and extended the open foil package to him. The student looked at Broad and then back at the smoked salmon before pinching off a portion of the pink fillet.

"Go ahead, pass it around to your classmates," Dowg whispered, knowing that the smoked aroma was permeating the room. "It's good form anyway," he added slyly.

The fish was passed around among the students, and soon most had quit listening to Broad and were enjoying the authentic alder-smoked taste. Having distracted the class while Broad droned on, Dowg began to softly whistle between suppressed chuckles.

Looking up at the sounds, Broad finally noticed Dowg pointing his middle finger, not up, but right at him, and laughing with his bright eyes brought nearly to tears.

"Seems to me your professor's boring reading of his own writing has become a waste of your time young people!" Dowg said theatrically standing up. "I'm sorry your tuition dollars go to professors who talk without end! Beware students, of the cobwebs and labyrinths of words and arguments constructed by philosophers," Dowg cautioned. "For they force us to unlearn what was not worth trying to learn in the first place! I hope that you all enjoyed the fish!" he concluded with a smile and nod before he exited the classroom, and the door shut behind him with a loud click.

Dowg arrived at *Weekly Seminar* just in time to see Metro organizing his thoughts and computer files for his presentation. Seeing the title *How Music Makes Sex Better: The Relationships among Music, Touch, and Arousal,* Dowg decided to lie comfortably in his usual place on the steps in the way.

Metro, feeling more nervous speaking to a group than playing music for one, read nearly word-for-word the presentation put on numerous PowerPoint slides. After a very long time, Dowg became bored and focused his thoughts on reading an editorial from *The CU Independent* he had snatched from a recycling bin.

Dowg had read most of the editorial when he noted that Metro had paused in his seemingly never-ending presentation. Dowg looked up at the big screen to see a blank slide on Metro's presentation with no writing on it.

"Cheer up everyone!" Dowg bellowed for all attendees to hear. "There's land in sight!"

"You're a dog," Broad said to him flatly.

"Quite true," Dowg replied as if it was a self-evident actuality that Broad had somehow overlooked.

"I return again and again to help those who have sold me out," Dowg explained, "but I am a breed that is praised in hunting. Many fear fatigue if they venture out hunting with me, so you do not accept me for who I am because you are too afraid of the discomforts of the hunting lifestyle. Which perfectly explains why pansy puff professor types like you produce entitlement-minded little snowflakes that melt down when triggered by simple truths or good humor. Wouldn't want to offend anyone with a provoking thought or intelligent joke, now would we, professor?"

Dowg kept on, his eyes growing brighter, "Isn't it strange Broad, that in your beloved bastion of higher education and indoctrination, comedians and controversial thinkers or speakers are banned or driven from campus? You PC pansy-ass virtue signaling do-gooder Marxists need to wake up, grow up, and for everyone's sake, toughen up! More importantly, stop assailing freedom of speech! Your intolerances are a genuine disservice to all liberty-loving free-thinkers who question authority, especially yours Broad," Dowg barked before growling again.

"If your precious little entitlement-minded snowflakes can't compete in the realm of ideas running with the big dogs, then show them their place under the porch Broad. Maybe call it a *Safe Zone*, provide cookies and crayons and talk only puppies and posies. For best effect, ban all speaking of life's harsh and beautiful truths with any frail-brained buttercup; they'll wilt from the glare of the facts," he stated without pausing for breath. "If possible, provide *Cry Rooms* for them to recover and to re-construct themselves in the smoky shroud of identity politics. Think group! Group think! It'll be great! Go Buffs!"

Dowg kept barking, without giving Broad a chance to reply.

"Do you find it strange, Broad, that professor types such as yourself should investigate the ills of the figures of history while these professors are ignorant of their own ills?" he asked without any sarcasm. "Or do you find it strange that music professors can tune the strings of a guitar while leaving the dispositions of their own souls in discord riding their emotional rollercoasters of finicky feelings? Or that astronomy professors can theorize and gaze at the planets, moons and stars, while they overlook the important matters at hand?"

A small crowd of students and professors had gathered around the two men. Taking advantage, Dowg addressed them.

"If ever there was a word that has been perverted, it would be the word *education*. I prefer a sort of ignorance of your modern-day *education*. Not ignorance as not knowing anything but ignorance as in a sense of dispensing with unnecessary learning and acquiring only knowledge that is sufficient for a good and simple life.

"Learning and education are indeed the foundations on which a good and happy life are built, but only if oriented in the right direction," Dowg said glancing at the student faces surrounding him. "Beware that your education is nothing more than job conditioning for automaton slavery in corrupt market places that require blind obedience. In only those forms of learning that help people live a natural and simple life can true education be found. Broad, your modern prison system posing as an education system merely controls the young, consoles the old, and adorns the rich," Dowg concluded.

UNC's Roberta Lichter, who had received her PhD under the tutelage of Broad at CU, listened to Dowg's diatribe and criticisms. She took offense at his snowflake and higher education railings and thus approached him.

"Dowg, you can be so ugly that nature would not have gone wrong if you had been born with the ears of a donkey."

Dowg displayed a wide, tooth-filled grin and formed his calm reply.

In a voice that mimicked Broad reading out loud he said, "Robbie, in the case of most men, their physical appearance

214

is not as important as their intelligence, whereas in the case of women like you, looks are of paramount importance because of your naturally occurring lack of intelligence."

Roberta turned red, scowled and scrunched her lips tightly, giving Dowg her most evil glare. Not too dissimilar actually from the arms-folded scowl she cast at Dr. Spencer in the picture.

"When we will we ever be free from Toxic Masculinity?" Roberta muttered to herself loud enough for Dowg to hear before she turned her back on him and walked off.

"Toxic masculinity?" He laughed, thinking how strange it was that a lesbian would use such an expression. Dowg had already found her guilty of appropriating many aspects of male culture. "Seems the only thing she lacks is a cock. Maybe she could use one," Dowg thought to himself. Aloud he said, "When we are free of your hate-filled Toxic Feminism?"

Roberta kept walking, increasing her pace.

"Samuel!" Dowg grinned at him, "Was it you that said that at the end of the debate, slander is the tool of the loser?"

Dowg howled with delight as he watched Roberta scurry out of the auditorium.

Chapter 21 - The Gathering of the Pack

It is no coincidence that howling has been a superior form of personal and mass communication among the wolf-descended predators. Whether in laughter or loss, they communicate honestly and transparently to the universe, including their prey and pack. No display of hunting skill, cohesive teamwork or the life of another goes uncelebrated. Cathartic for them, terrifying for their prey, their primal melodic voices remind every listener of their place in the chain of the good life, the wild life.

This held true for those gathering at Houndman's property on James Creek outside of Jamestown, Colorado. You may have seen similar scenes of men and dogs in November at the height of the rut and big game hunting. Camping gear, coolers, trucks and jeeps, cold weather wear and nearly as many humans as dogs filled Houndman's creekside property for the annual *Gathering of the Pack*.

Yes, it's true, all past and recent initiates who had passed Dowg's test for *"Hunt Club"* membership were gathered at the secluded **Swift Dog Gym**. We might agree that the *Army of the Dog* is not a typical secret society for good reasons. I've convinced the ADogs, or members of the *Army of the Dog*, that security and surveillance are no concern if the dogs outnumber the members. It is also true that the ADogs do not wear hooded costumes, display skulls or crosses, dance, or even light candles in dark, dank rooms. But they do dabble in bones.

The smell of smoked venison and elk wafted from Houndman's back porch to combine with the sounds of dogs at play in the cool of the afternoon. Members young and old, dogs included, greeted each other with the ADog handshake. Between greetings and running and leaping in play, the thirsty dogs made their way to the creek for a drink while their owners did the same with beers and spirits as various as their breeds and personalities. Some members were setting up their tents outside the pine bark mulched area of the gym while others sat in lawn chairs, engaged in very earnest and humorous conversation.

From the grill, Houndman pulled a mound of shiny, tin foiled baked potatoes, and from the grill's side burner, a heaping potful of barbeque baked beans. At the opposite end of the grill, an extra-large bowl of vinegar-based coleslaw sat patiently with a large spoon protruding from it. The *Gathering of the Pack* of ADogs began, as it always has, with a good meal of smoked game and time to catch up with old friends. Dowg enthusiastically introduced our three graduate students to the other ADogs, who welcomed them warmly into the *Army of the Dog*. Will couldn't recall having ever seen Dowg more animated; his eyes glowed more brightly, his spirit rejuvenated by the many dogs, some furry, some bipedal.

The meal was officially concluded when the dogs had licked clean all the paper plates, and they were put into a large paper bag, also containing some newspaper and copies of one of Broad's recent articles. Members organized their chairs, coolers and gear and got ready to camp the night at the gym. They pitched their tents outside the two large semicircles of firewood that were equidistant from the large stone-lined fire pit. Inside the pit, firewood was mounded around the base of a neatly-skinned pine timber that stood upright in the center of the fuel. The top half of the skinned timber had been hewn into the clear features of a large rodent, courtesy of Houndman's chainsaw. Sitting atop the timber, the beady-eyed, carved rodent looked solemnly down on them and the large, round stump set next to the fire pit.

At 6pm sharp, Houndman, with an Odell's IPA in hand, stood up on the stump, raised his head and gave a long and inviting howl. As he threw back his head to howl again, all members, including the dogs, joined in the unifying chorus. Jack's nubby little tail oscillated into an indiscernible blur as he pranced and danced on his little legs. He quivered with excitement at the howling of the Black and Tans, Foxhounds, Beagles, a Treeing Walker coonhound, two Redbones and the deep voice of a Bloodhound. Jack joined in the howling refrain along with the other sporting mutts and purebreds in attendance: from Golden and Labrador Retrievers to Terriers and Spaniels, their unified crescendo echoed from the creek bottom to the canyon beyond.

Club members gathered the excited dogs by their collars and stood outside the openings of the two semi-circles of mounded firewood. Standing equally distant from the firepit, the dogs tugged against their collars, whining, yelping and barking in frenzied anticipation. Houndman stepped off the stump toward the unlit firepit and looked at both ends of the semicircle mounds to ensure that no dog might gain an unfair advantage.

Reaching into the firepit, Houndman opened the door to an animal carrier and a large, bushy-tailed woodrat hesitantly emerged.

Hearing the yelps and barks of the anxious hounds, but unable to see them over the stones, the rat ran directly under the protection of the split wood in the fire pit. Producing a lighter from his pocket, Houndman lit the assembled paper and wood along several places of the base of the kindling teepee and then walked away when the smoke began to gently rise upward.

"May the *Swift Dog Scramble* begin!" Houndman yelled, "Cut 'em loose!"

The rat chose to escape the blaze and scale the firepit rocks in the direction of the eastern semicircle of firewood. Rapidly approaching were the longest-legged hounds in the lead from the northern and southern openings of the semicircles, each trying to gauge and cut off the rat's escape route to the wood mound. Pearly was in the lead from the southern opening and a young Saluki named Barguest from the northern one. Both hounds were in wide open sprints, bodies fully extended, feet only occasionally touching the ground. Jack knew he might be trampled by the larger dogs scrambling towards the rodent inside the large circled area, so he darted around the back of the eastern semicircle of firewood.

The woodrat went from a hurried scuttle to a distressed dash in its honest effort to reach the eastern semicircle. The ADogs watched as their various dogs closed in on the running rodent, each wondering if this would be the year the outcome of the *Swift Dog Scramble* was determined by sheer speed alone. Will and Aldo stepped closer to see, both calculating quickly in their minds with me the probabilities of the race's finish.

Same for the lead hounds, Pearly and Barguest; they were doing the same geometric calculations of distance and time in their brains with me, only faster than the men. Realizing that they would not capture their prey, and that they were unable to come to a complete stop, I told Pearly to jump cleanly over the eastern semicircle of wood, and I advised Barguest to apply his padded brakes and skid to a halt.

Upon arrival of the entire pack, young and old alike, every dog put its nose to the ground and the wood. Jack, the smallest of the pack, worked his way further into the pile, his little nubby tail wagging wildly each time a dog removed a piece of wood with its paws or jaws. At each change of the rat's hiding place, the dogs jumped, whined, yipped and snorted loudly through noses buried in the wood pile.

It was not long before the rat came to the end of the semicircle of mounded protection; he was completely surrounded. The rat could see that only a little wood and several inches separated it from the jaws and paws of the determined Jack Russell. The rat called on me when Jack was so close it could smell elk meat on the breath of the terrifying terrier. I convinced the rat to play the odds by avoiding Jack and making a mad dash out of the dwindling pile. Aiming to shoot the gap of the northern entrance to the protection of the second semicircle of wood, the rat darted past Ol' Cassee and a beagle of about the same age. For a moment, it appeared that the juking and jiving rat would reach the safety of the wood pile, but a large paw belonging to a Redbone Coonhound named Rummy halted the rat's progress.

Rummy, short for Verum, quickly applied his powerful jaws to the rat and shook his head with fierce force and spectacular speed. The rat let out its last squeals in a flurry of tearing flesh, broken bones and punctured organs. The other dogs watched, panting as Rummy proudly displayed his harvest with head held high in a supremely beautiful strut around the wood; this year's winner of the *Swift Dog Scramble.*

After the parade and loud applause, Rummy dropped the lifeless rodent at Houndman's feet. Houndman picked up the dead rat and threw it into the blazing flames of the firepit. He then raised his head and gave another long and lonesome howl, in which all canine and human attendees joined him, all enjoying the smell of burning rat flesh that temporarily filled the evening air.

In exchange for the rat, Houndman pulled from a large cooler a raw elk steak for Rummy, who inhaled it with minimal chewing and maximum tail wagging. From the same cooler, Houndman pulled various bones of recently harvested deer and elk for the dogs to enjoy as the evening cooled, the fire crackled and the beers flowed among the ADogs.

As was customary, attendees took to their seats around the fire pit as each dog worked a bone in the dancing light of the flames. Houndman strode to the large stump near the firepit and ascended it for all to hear and see him.

"Death to dishonesty!" he shouted with a raised fist.

"Death to dishonesty!" they shouted back.

"Long live Reason!" he shouted raising his fist again.

"Long live Reason!" we shouted back.

"Long run the *Army of the Dog*!" he shouted.

"Long run the *Army of the Dog!*" they shouted back ending with howling, yipping, barking, and chortling.

As was customary, the remainder of the evening was devoted to *Hunting with ADogs* stories when members shared the circumstances of their motivations for hunting specific prey. In keeping with their society's traditions, Houndman first drew attention to the new pups of the pack. Official introductions for Will, Aldo and Ben were met with barking and yips from the humans that only temporarily distracted the dogs from their bones. Will took to the stump first where he explained his cause with the banking industry, how it affected his family, and what action was taken, including Dowg's big bank deposit. To the yowls and laughter of the members, our graduate student puppies shared their stories, making sure to include their adventures "hunting" with Dowg.

As the night wore on, and the dogs worked their bones in the firelight, ADog members of various ages took to the stump to tell of their own hunting experiences. Some of the older members spoke of burning and blowing up buildings and dams, while others spoke of leading marches, organizing petitions and speaking publicly. Some told of rendering excavation and drilling equipment useless while a few spoke of working from within the system to hound white-collar thieves, politicians, pedophiles, pimps and war criminals. Even Dowg took the stump to tell the story of his biking adventures in Target. He stepped off the stump to a chorus of applause and a combination of laughter and howling before yielding it to another good friend and longtime member of the pack.

"Sentiment without action is the ruin of the soul!" bayed the tall old ADog atop the stump. He wore a broad-brimmed hat, a sardonic grin, and cigar ash on his pants. Yes, it's true, these words pierced through the three students' beer-soaked and whisky-marinated brains like a shotgun blast of bright light into a mind cave, ricocheting repeatedly off the cranium walls until fully lit inside. I even helped Will make the connection between these men, these ADogs, and the words inscribed in the stone on the back wall of his earthen den. At that moment, in the glow of the fire, Will understood. Some of these men were his predecessors in the den. They had trained at the ***Swift Dog Gym***, cut and split wood, lived Spartan, passed initiation and come out of the den into the light as men of action.

I convinced Will, Ben and Aldo that night that Dowg had not gone mad in the least, and that it is indeed true -- being a real man means that you're a *man of action*. They are not billowing hot air from an overworked pie hole, they are not fountains of empty gibberish or the ringmasters of semantic circle jerks, you'll know them because they are *men of action*.

The tall old ADog atop the stump patiently puffed his cigar before reporting that the politicians of the mighty Republic of Boulder County had sold out to big gas and oil.

They would be fracking in Boulder County Open Spaces.

Low, but clearly audible growls from the men around the fire stirred the dogs from their bones in the firelight. Barguest and Rummy barked viciously at the unseen intruder. Pearly put her nose to the air, and Jack looked directly at the old ADog atop the stump taking a draw from his lit cigar. Jack studied him closely and wagged his nub slowly trying to discern what sort of adventure would come from this proclamation that made the ADogs growl.

As was the customary tradition, they howled late into the night in their most sincere effort to find those elusive truths often buried near the bottom of Houndman's handle of Gentleman Jack Daniels whiskey.

Chapter 22 - Person of Interest – Dowg Interrogation #2

When the Boulder Police arrived for Dowg, he had shifted locations and was on his knees begging for cash, before a popularly used ATM; already a small crowd had gathered, mostly behind him.

"What are you doing?" an impatient voice asked from the group, obviously in line to withdraw cash.

"I'm developing my strength of character by being rejected," Dowg replied, still fixed on his goal of obtaining a good workout using a lifeless machine, even when the officers arrived.

At the police station, Dowg found himself seated once again in the same interrogation room with the same Special Agent, H. Mortimer Bennett with the same Colorado Bureau of Investigation.

"Let me guess – the bureau of super sleuths needs me to verify that I am me in a picture that I have already verified I am in as me? Shouldn't you be trying to fill some quota or collude with some federal agency in the cover-up of a mass shooting?" Dowg asked.

With a half-hearted smirk born of some appreciation for Dowg's humor, but mostly irritated, Investigator Bennett opened a file folder and slid the same picture across the table to him that he'd viewed during the last interrogation.

"We have good reason to believe that there are other accomplices who aided Damon and Melissa in the shootings," Bennett stated, pointing to the bottom left corner of the picture at Melissa next to Dr. Guarneri and Damon behind the pillar.

"What makes you so sure?" Dowg asked again looking over the picture.

"Can you tell me anything about the man whose hand is on Anthony's shoulder? That *is* Anthony, in the blue there in the lower left corner with the open book and vines around his head?" Investigator Bennett asked, ignoring Dowg's question.

Dowg paused briefly while he looked. "It's too dark, I can't make out his face," Dowg replied squinting. "Looks suspicious to me though, probably another vegetarian hippie pacifist. Better raid his home, score a blacklisted book or bag of granola, maybe even a Grateful Dead or Leftover Salmon album. Beware of his fruit dehydrator; it's probably one of those dirty nuclear bombs –I recommend looking into it."

"Can you tell me anything about this young, shirtless man in the leftmost of the picture? The one running with documents in his hands?" Bennett asked.

"I can't see his face nor can I put a name to it," Dowg said after looking again at the picture, "but I'm confident he is another one of those communications or law professor know-it-alls bent on wordplay and public speaking. As disingenuous as they are clever with their words, I would rather slam my dick in the door than discuss an important matter with anyone of those shyster-headed lawyers afflicted with diarrhea of the mouth. Oddly enough, Broad and I (he poked at Broad's face in the picture) actually agree on this matter, which means that shirtless slick talker just might just be your man," Dowg satisfactorily concluded with a grin.

"About this man Samuel here," the agent said leaning over to point to the thick man in green conversing with Halsey in the middle left of the picture. "We have been made aware by the Department of Justice that Samuel has refused to provide evidence against one Mr. Leon Salamis for anti-Semitic and other forms of hate speech involving his opposition to the current U.S. administration. Do you have any information about Samuel's motives or methods to aid young people in an attempted overthrow of the US government?"

"Oh Yes! The Department of Justifying Corporate Injustices – 'if it's too big to fail, it's too big to jail!' – Now there's an institution every American can trust! Best devote resources to hunting down a dancing pacifist living a simple life in a tiny house with a large complainer for a wife," Dowg snorted. "Seems to me his greatest crime and contribution to society has been toying with people's minds and words to expose their ignorance by reasoning clearly. I think he should be rewarded for his contributions to society and for the consistency of his message."

"What's his message?"

Dowg paused only momentarily. "In my words, it would be to firmly grasp your head and pull it out of your ignorant ass to live a life of virtue if you want to be a happy person," Dowg grinned, nodding his head in agreement at his crude, simple-sentence summary of Samuel's message.

"These young men on the bottom right with Dr. Schwede," the investigator said, pointing to the picture, "they seem to be good pals; would they be involved or aid in the attempted overthrow of the US government?"

"Those boys I believe are mostly engineers," Dowg answered immediately, "And I know Dr. Schwede is no pansy puff pretend professor; his brain works overtime and produces, and he expects the same out of his students. Those baby faces don't seem old enough to know to drink good beer." Dowg continued to stare at the picture.

"Who knows, maybe they gather and worship some number or engineer of old or an engineering software of the day? They might even talk about Freemasonry temples while under the psychoactive effects of Pabst Blue Ribbon, dancing around in their undies with their hoodies on their heads."

Investigator Bennett scowled. "Are there any other secret societies among the individuals in this picture?"

"Who knows what Broad and his cronies might be up to? Last I heard he was collaborating with some other academic nut jobs at Syracuse University to establish a society of their own."

"Then there is Robbie, there near the center, scowling at Dr. Spencer," Dowg said, flicking her image with his finger. "A true ringmistress of the lesbian mafia or what I've heard some call the *Secret Society of Man-Haters*. I call them *The Lickety Splits*; others call them higher education administrators. Always trying to rectify the inequalities of the past by treating people unfairly today." Dowg shook his head. "Worse, their stranglehold on higher education will ensure that they confuse many young people to attempt the same disservice for others. Is it legal to chase such silly myths as equality or the equality of outcome? Might want to check into the *Secret Society of Man-Haters,* Mortimer. But be sure you don't open a door for them, or ma'am them; they've been liberated and enlightened you know," Dowg advised.

Before the investigator could speak, Dowg frowned and continued. "What confuses me the most about this picture is the baby, the boy and the little she-man or he-woman in drag there - the one all in white. Has the bureau of super snoopers been able to identify this individual?" Dowg looked up from the picture to pin his steady gaze on Bennett.

The special agent hesitated slightly before answering. "We're not certain of the identity of the baby, boy and young person in white. Our analyses revealed that they may be related to the deceased artist, Sanzio Urban."

"As in his siblings?" Dowg inspected the artist's face on the far right of the picture; he is the only one of the group looking at the camera. And then Dowg looked more closely at the faces of the baby and boy on the bottom left and then at the face of the person in white.

"Or as in Sanzio himself?" Dowg asked almost to himself before returning his gaze to the investigator, who said nothing in reply.

"Seems to me you have a person of interest here in the unidentified pretty boy? Superimposed images, out of time, and in drag—we just might be looking at the she-male aid to revolutionaries that you're after!" Dowg concluded with notable optimism, and even some certainty, at having possibly identified a person of interest.

Chapter 23 – Field Dress

Investigator Bennett stayed on the hunt for any accomplices, still perplexed by the unidentified young person in white and still unsure of the sex of the individual. This can complicate hunting, even if only for deer, for which Halsey and our graduate students had only two distinguishable sexes to identify: buck or doe. On this particular hunt, the tag was for a doe.

Anthony wrote Halsey that Glen Haven's Fire Chief had a doe tag to fill for the season and could use some help. Having suffered a broken back in a fall, he couldn't work, hunt or perform the usual chores associated with family and mountain living.

"I'll take care of it!" Halsey replied.

"Not that I condone the killing and eating of those beautiful creatures," Anthony responded, "but it would be a big help to the chief and his family. Feel free to stay at the Inn. Don't fear gawds –AC."

Halsey awakened Aldo, Will and Ben at 4:30AM to begin their journey through the early morning darkness to their vantage point. At the Glen Haven General Store, they crossed the bridge onto the dirt road along the North Fork of the Big Thompson. At its confluence with Fox Creek, they veered left to walk along the small stream approximately half-mile to four cabins sitting along the stream's edge. Damaged by flooding, falling trees, and a lack of care, the old gray-brown tin roofed cabins served as their landmark to turn off-road and head up the mountainside.

They ascended briefly through a small meadow surrounded by the ever present Ponderosa pines, passing the still visible rock and concrete foundations of a dilapidated cabin from the late 1800s. They intersected a trail used by the Glen Haven locals, including Dowg and his pack on Wednesdays, and climbed west into US Forest Service lands. No one spoke during the hike, and all headlamps were on dim settings, per Halsey's request to be quiet and inconspicuous. Will fell only once trudging upward when he slipped on a pocket of shaded frozen snow to land in a patchwork of currant bushes that mostly broke his fall.

Making good time and staying moving, they reached their high rock vantage point. The party came to a stop on a large rock with a flat overhang big enough to accommodate their bodies and gear. Quietly in the dark, Halsey turned off his headlamp, pulled off his pack and began to ready his rifle from its case. Our graduate students shed their packs and pulled out wool blankets to lie on as they waited for the November sun to rise. As their body heat from the climb dissipated, the cold of the morning settled on the group. Will lay on his back staring into the darkness of the unlit sky and attempting to sleep in 20 something degrees.

When the rays of sunlight woke the morning, Will rolled over onto his stomach to see Halsey, laid out flat on his stomach and peering over the edge. Next to him his rifle rested comfortably in its open case. From their vantage point, they could see the North Fork drainage to their backs and the Fox Creek drainage to the front. The crows flying in the early morning sun could see the hunting party and commented on their presence, especially Halsey's large 7mm bolt-action rifle.

Halsey looked through the scope, and the students through their binoculars, at the various life forms getting about the start of the chilly morning. They caught a glimpse of a red fox that had startled a mountain cotton tail, which darted from under a mature cedar tree to its network of holes under rocks and roots. The trees were coming alive with chickadees, blue jays, and nuthatches sharing the piney resources with Red, Eastern Fox and Abert's tassel-eared squirrels. They could hear plainly the warning whistle of a marmot and the gobbling of wild turkeys as they foraged for their morning meals near Fox Creek. The unmistakable echo of the downy woodpecker hammering away at an old snag reminded Halsey of well-timed bursts of machine gun fire.

They continued sunning themselves in the light of the new day on their rock perch while they watched and listened with minimal moving and no speaking. Aldo and Halsey spotted a mule buck at about the same time, first by the emergence of a black nose, white muzzle and then a white rump patch around a white tail with a black tip.

Looking through his scope, Halsey noted the large tines of the male's horns were composed of two upward angled beams that forked twice into four points. Handsome buck, ought to be females nearby, he thought to himself, focusing on the direction of the buck's advance.

He was right. One, then another two mule does were soon visible among the outlying trees of a grassy bald, delicately picking their way across a small side canyon that sloped towards Fox Creek. Will could see the deer with his naked eye and estimated the distance to be about five or six football fields away, or 632 yards according to Aldo's range finder optic reading.

Flat on their stomachs, they waited and watched the deer and their direction of travel along the slopes parallel with the creek. Yes, it's true, I have had many conversations with all types of prey, including hoofed mammals, on how best to travel, stay aware and avoid predators by stopping, looking, listening, and eating with varying head movements. Even for some of your kind, a trusty and well-placed head fake could save the day or score some points.

After disappearing into the narrow of a thickly-wooded drainage, the does reemerged on the crest, still at the same stop-look-listen pace. They grazed cautiously, lifting their heads often to look around. Their big ears twitched as they listened for any danger.

Aldo's optic reading showed 398 yards away.

Ben and Will noticed Halsey's right index finger touch the trigger guard, then press the safety, then back to the trigger guard as he remained motionless on his stomach. Ben thought about plugging his ears but looked on as Halsey waited patiently for the largest doe to stop and turn broad side.

The thunderous report of the 7mm rifle shook the air, rocks and eardrums of all life forms within the entire Fox Creek watershed.

The necessary time passed for the projectile to reach the target. "Just high," Aldo whispered seeing the bullet kick up dirt and rocks through his optics. The does appeared confused about the origin of the thunder stick and stood motionless, watching the buck bound off.

Halsey muttered an inaudible expletive; he quickly ejected the spent casing and bolted in a live round. We agreed that he misjudged the drop in altitude from his position to that of the doe's and that he would aim lower. The most mature doe faced them almost directly with her large floppy ears fully extended on an erect head and neck, still as stone, confused.

The second thunderclap of Halsey's rifle again roared its message throughout the nearby canyons. Again Aldo, Will and Ben watched and waited for the bullet to complete the distance. Upon impact, it knocked her back violently, off of her feet, to land on her side and back. The party continued watching, the ringing in their ears humming intensely, and noted that the doe did not rise.

They propped the deer on her back, with her head uphill, and organized rocks under her shoulders and hips. Once steadied, Aldo withdrew a long, stainless steel buck knife with a sawback and gently inserted the blade between the hind legs, just under the hide. Here he made one long incision, careful to circumvent the udder, up her soft underbelly. Aldo continued the incision to the jawbone using his fingers to separate the tissue and being careful not to cut through the muscle layer. Turning his knife to the sawback side, he separated the ribcage to open the chest cavity.

Ben took a step back at the first waft of air from the cavity. Despite the smell, Aldo thanked Halsey for making a good, clean shot through vital organs as opposed to the stomach.

Next, he severed the windpipe and connective tissues holding the interior organs to the diaphragm. After Will and Ben adjusted the stones from under her shoulders and hips, Aldo pulled out the entrails towards the pelvic region. With the majority of the organs pulled outside of the carcass, Aldo sawed through the pelvis and cut out the anus and sphincter muscles and removed the remaining entrails. Here, we would probably agree that if Houndman and

Dowg were in attendance, they might find a few useful metaphors for Broad.

Aldo wiped the blade of the large knife free of hair, meat, bones and tissue at the same time Halsey spotted a large wind-fallen pine that had sheared off the branches of an even larger neighboring relative. Ben fetched a thick, fallen branch which he broke to length by prying the smaller end of the branch between two large boulders. Halsey smoothed the ends of the sturdy wood by knocking the smaller branches off using a stone. Then he produced a big fixed-blade combat knife to smooth the ends of the round, bark-covered wood.

Will and Ben held the limb on each end, just above the deer's chest, while Halsey and Aldo used rope to lash her legs together, around, and to, the large and sturdy branch. With the excess rope slack, Halsey tied the deer's head to her front legs so as not to drag them on the ground or hit rocks and bushes. Once secured, Will and Ben wrapped their wool blankets around each end of the timber and readied their footing. On the count of three, the two hoisted the large branch onto their shoulders. With the deer hanging between them, the party hiked in the direction Halsey showed them.

Each took their turn at the front and the back of the long limb on their shoulders, packing their harvest out along the game trails. They descended the mountainside until they came upon a well-used single-track trail from which they hiked the deer to the fire chief's house. On a firmly-secured timber fastened to two trees, they hung the deer by her hind quarters using a large metal hanger that ran through both knees and kept her legs spread.

Halsey proceeded to skin the deer by cutting and firmly pulling the hairy hide from the muscular frame down to her head, which he severed with his combat knife. In keeping with his hunting and military traditions, Halsey quickly pondered a souvenir from his kill. Since there were no antlers, he simply cut her legs off at the knees and tossed one to each student.

Chapter 24 - WNS – November

It wasn't until the hunters had napped and spent an afternoon engaged in marksmanship and beermanship, that WNS attendees began arriving. Houndman was the first, in his old Ford F-150 stuffed with firewood, a cooler of elk meat and beer, and the smoker, all neatly stowed in the bed of the truck. In the back of the extended cab, Cassee and Pearly each looked out a side window while Jack stood on the seat between Houndman and Dowg in the front, doing his best to see over the dashboard.

The rusty doors of the old truck swung open with a squeak, and the dogs piled out and greeted the hunters at the Inn, sniffing and licking their deer-scented wear and hands. Jack's stubby nub wagged with speedy excitement, and he snorted through his nose, taking in the deer smell and tastes with his tongue. Pearly insisted on an ADog shake from all four hunters where she smelled and tasted of their hands. Upon completion of the usual required formalities, they gave each dog a fresh, organic tartar-fighting deer leg from the morning harvest.

"Happy Wednesday all," Anthony said emerging from the Glen Haven Inn to great the meat eaters. "I just wanted to let you Bambi slayers know that I have some guests

243

arriving this evening." He paused, "They aren't the usual Wednesday attendees." It was clear that he was insinuating that they be civil and hospitable to the outsiders.

"No Zeno this afternoon?" Houndman asked.

"No, he is delivering a speech at a memorial in Boulder this evening honoring Colorado victims of the tyranny of the 30 corporations, mostly the gas and oil industry," Anthony replied, "and seems he may have mentioned something about a statue dedication for the City of Boulder."

Will had set up the smoker and was watching the small wisps of smoke choose their scattered paths towards the atmosphere when Broad and Samuel arrived. Will noted the following stickers on Broad's back window and bumper:

Socialism – because people matter more than profits.

Sharing is caring.

Keep Left.

Karl Marx Is My Homeboy.

Hate Socialism? Buy Your Own Road.

Samuel was the first to ease his thick, large frame from the little Subaru.

"Seems that Broad is a little queasy from the canyon drive up Hwy 36; can one of you fetch a trash can or container for him? I'm afraid he's about to vomit," Samuel said over the roof of the car. Broad's door opened slightly.

Houndman, acting quickly, grabbed the metal waste container near the smoker and glided down the steps. He placed it next to Broad, who was still sitting in the car seat and spitting on the ground. Houndman watched Broad convulse twice before he vomited twice with two great heaves into the trash can.

After Broad spit twice more and regained himself from the nausea, Houndman leaned and peered into the vomit-splattered trash can.

"I see your lunch. And what looks like some bile, but I don't see your conceited pride in here Broad," Houndman said thoughtfully, but with visible disappointment, before taking another look inside the trash can to find it.

"Don't give up my friend!" Dowg proclaimed loudly from the deck trying to cheer up Houndman. "There is still hope for the ride home!"

Houndman and Samuel helped Broad up the stairs for a seat in the cool, fresh air of the sunny November afternoon.

Halsey gave Samuel a hearty embrace and a slap on his meaty shoulder before pouring him a glass of wine. Halsey sensed that something didn't seem right with Samuel, and that it wasn't likely Broad's vomiting. Houndman listened in while he assembled the kindling to be lit in the chiminea. Next to him, Ol' Cassee worked her deer leg, wagging her tail at the sight of Samuel.

"Are you doing all right, Samuel?"

"I couldn't be better," Samuel said softly. "As you know, my leadership consulting services business is doing well, although I could probably charge my clients more." He was still clearly struggling with the decision, but there seemed to be something else distracting him.

"And the wife and kids?" Halsey asked, grinning a little. "All's well on the home front?"

"Surly as ever."

"Anything else Samuel?" Broad asked, the color slowly returning to his never-smiling face.

Samuel paused momentarily to choose his words. "As you may know, the 30 tyrant corporations are likely to be swept from power in the next election, given the intense unrest of the American people. And it appears that some are saying that I am associated with these American oligarchs and their corporate rule. A former student of mine is actually one of the 30 CEOs and the head of a large media corporation. But I'm not convinced that makes me responsible for his actions or decisions."

"Who did you piss off this time?" Houndman asked with a large smile.

"I may have ridiculed someone deserving of it."

"I find no fault in calling things by their proper name," Dowg interjected.

"Sounds like a damn witch hunt to me," Houndman proclaimed with a frown and furled brow. "Are they taking you to court?"

"Possibly."

"On what charges?"

"I don't know yet; it may depend on who is in power," Samuel said. He was calm and collected, as if it was all just a silly game. Broad shook his head slowly from side to side.

Hearing the hum of tires slowing on pavement, attendees looked to see Dr. Spencer arriving in his Land Rover Discovery. Only two bumper stickers adorned it: *Facts Matter* and *SCIENCE. It works, BITCHES*.

Spencer stepped out of the tall vehicle. The physician was neatly-groomed and smartly dressed as if he'd just stepped off the cover of *Outdoor Magazine*. Similar to many residents of Fort Collins and the mighty Republic, he wore expensive but highly functional outdoor wear; he preferred the Patagonia and North Face brands. A gold signet ring glittered on his right hand in the November sunlight and in the other flashed a bottle of Book Cliff Vineyards Crescendo.

"Gentlemen!" he called, waving to them as he made his way up the steps.

"Would you like a beer?" Dowg said, pulling a Laughing Lab Scottish Ale from the cooler for the CSU professor.

Although he preferred wine over beer, Spencer took the bottle anyway and held it up high to the light to inspect its color. "You're true to form, Dowg, thank you as always," he said handing the beer back to him with a smile.

"It's good to see you all at your leisure," Dr. Spencer noted, scanning the faces on the deck and taking in a strong whiff of the mesquite smoke, beer and mountain air.

"Ah, leisure! My most valuable possession indeed!" Samuel replied with a nod of his head, clearly signifying that it was no small matter.

"And a very dangerous possession for the ignorant," Broad said. "Play for the young is essential, but the state must be careful to protect the masses from imagination, symbols, mythology or any form of uncertain thinking that would occur in leisure. For example, poets left to their leisure are more likely to confuse themselves and others, never mind historians or other artists that distract the ignorant masses."

"I have also published on the topic of leisure," Spencer followed, "and take a very different position to Broad's, which is yet again both untenable and unnatural. Leisure and its proper use are of utmost importance for all people, of any class. I maintain that leisure is among our greatest goods and among our highest callings to action and virtue. This will best produce cohesive communities bounded by reason and civility."

Spencer continued. "As I have argued, the proper use of leisure is directly associated with positive outcomes that bring true and meaningful happiness rather than fleeting moments of pleasure. But this can only occur if the populace is not distracted by obsessions with simple amusements and diversions from work. True happiness from leisure is rooted in immersed action and the pursuit of excellence." He paused. "Furthermore, I would argue that the improper use of leisure by a society in a time of peace and prosperity will likely be its undoing. It can make men lazy and amusement-minded and turned away from any true confrontation with ourselves. It's the stuff of learning and action, not mind-numbing TV and pointless shopping."

"Bravo, Spencer!" Dowg shouted, "*To action in our leisure!*" he said thrusting his fist into the air.

Pearly, lying next to him and grinding away at her deer leg, wagged her tail in obvious agreement. She gently rolled onto her back with the bone in her mouth and raised a paw so Dowg could scratch her belly.

Houndman smiled, stoked the chiminea with small end cuts of wood and blew gently on the fire to revive the flames.

"Dowg," Broad said suddenly, gazing at the now brightly-burning chiminea, "whatever became of your family after the infamous banking scandal with your father?" He purposely raised his voice for a change. He wanted to be sure the others heard.

"Damn, the little prick has come out to play," Houndman muttered to himself turning to see Dowg's blue eyes darken with anger.

"How come you never discuss what became of your mother?" Broad inquired, still just loud enough for others to hear. Dowg's eyes darkened more, but before he could retort, Metro broke in. His bland, handsome face seemed shocked.

"You were involved in a banking scandal?" Metro asked, setting down his guitar and looking at Dowg. "Shouldn't you be in prison or paying people back their money?"

Dowg flushed red, digging deep to deal with his anger at Metro's ignorance of the scandal in which Dowg and his father had been accused of producing a counterfeit currency and engaging in a conspiracy against the U.S. They had, in fact, developed an alternative currency by minting a "Liberty" coin and issuing a paper currency backed by precious metals, that according to Federal prosecutors, competed with the US Dollar. Dowg rarely, if ever, spoke of it or his background to anyone.

"Metro, that was a time when I was much like you are now; but such as I am now, you will never be, soy boy." Dowg worked to suppress the flames in his eyes. Pearly and Jack, sensing Dowg's displeasure, abandoned their deer legs for a moment and watched him closely.

Backing quickly away from the flaring topic, Metro retrieved his guitar and began to pick and strum some bluegrass. Tension eased, the humans resumed their drinking, and the dogs lay enjoying the fire. Dowg stared into the fire, his thoughts far away in a different time and place. He absently scratched Pearly's ears, and she thumped her tail on the deck in thanks, looking him directly in the eyes.

Broad and Spencer went back to their discussion on work and inequality, and soon, Houndman and Anthony pronounced supper ready. Anthony's guests started the food line inside where he had been roasting red potatoes with olive oil and rosemary. Next to the starch was a brimming bowl of braised red cabbage and onions with fresh carrots. And for the carnivores, a smoked elk roast covered in garlic that Aldo had carved neatly into slender pink slices.

Attendees ate their meals in the warmth of the Inn where Houndman had also built and maintained a fire in the large stone fireplace. It was mostly a WNS evening of light conversation about the impending semester's end, projects, papers and the steady accumulation of final exam anxiety. Finishing their dessert of apple and nut salad with agave, Samuel and the meat-eaters stepped outside onto the deck where Houndman once again revived the chiminea. Dowg warmed the dogs by rubbing their flanks vigorously. Halsey and the young ADogs warmed themselves using the reliable antifreeze properties of whiskey from a flask.

"Have you ever asked yourself the question: *What is a good life?*" Samuel asked, purposefully sparking discussion as the group settled into the Adirondack chairs surrounding the fire. Will, Ben and Aldo discussed this question and explored with Samuel the criteria that should or should not be applied, including the importance of knowledge in answering this question. Before they had even opened another beer, Samuel had convinced them that they knew nothing.

"I don't know shit either," Samuel said bluntly. "But a life of not checking shit out is not really worth living, so we must try to know shit about ourselves. I've come to the firm conclusion that I don't know shit – with the one exception – that I know that I don't know shit. The only good shit out there is knowledge, the only bad shit is ignorance. On the whole, if people didn't take shit to excess and were content with the shit they had, they probably wouldn't lead such unhappy lives."

No shit. No gawds necessary, no gawd fear required, Will thought to himself, grinning a little and staring into the fire, pondering the words of the beefy leadership consultant.

"Speaking of excess, where is Halsey?" Samuel asked, standing up and scanning the deck for him.

No Halsey.

Knowing his friend well, Samuel stood up and made his way to the back of the Inn to check the hot tub. Samuel stopped and his face grew stern at the site of Halsey in the hot tub with one of Anthony's lady guests.

Here we go again, Samuel thought to himself. Although he had a wife at home, Halsey was known to stray whenever the opportunity presented itself. He wished Halsey could sport a little more virtue in resisting the temptations of women.

At the moment, Halsey was fully lip-locked with the woman sitting on his lap in the hot tub oblivious to anything but their small, heated pool of passion. With his arms wrapped around her, Halsey's big fingers fumbled with the small knot of her bathing suit top.

Mission accomplished. He took a swig of whisky from his omnipresent flask before plunging his face between her large, smooth, semi-submerged breasts. Halsey didn't find any virtue between them, and being fairly drunk, he felt no pain during his underwater explorations. His second brain was large and in charge of the thinking, and Halsey didn't see Samuel approach.

"Halsey! Let's. Get. Movin!"

Samuel stepped towards the hot tub startling the woman, who clung firmly to Halsey, seemingly frightened by the thick, unattractive man whose bull neck blended into a solid mass of iron muscle and steel nerves.

"Ah... Uh... Sam?" Halsey slurred slightly, opening his bloodshot eyes and slowly grinning, "You can't see that I'm tending to some important business right here, right now?"

"Let's go Halsey," Samuel said again, calmly reaching for the married man's arm. "These sensual pleasures will destroy you, my friend."

Chapter 25 - The Thirty Tyrants

1. Alphabet Incorporated

2. Amazon

3. AT&T

4. Bank of America

5. BP Shell

6. Cargill

7. CBS Corporation

8. Citibank

9. Coca-Cola

10. Comcast Corporation

11. Corrections Corporation of America

12. Dow Chemical

13. DynCorp

14. Exxon Mobil

15. Gilead Sciences

16. GlaxoSmithKline

17. Goldman Sachs

18. Halliburton Corporation

19. Johnson and Johnson

20. Lockheed Martin

21. Monsanto

22. Nestle

23. News Corporation

24. Northrop Grumman

25. Pfizer

26. Raytheon

27. Smithfield Foods

28. United States Federal Reserve Bank

29. Verizon

30. Viacom

Chapter 26 – The Last Seminar

Will and Aldo strolled across CU's Boulder campus with Dr. Schwede to the last *Weekly Seminar* of December, also the last seminar for the fall semester. Opening one of several doors to a large ballroom, which served as their auditorium, they entered to the hum of conversations, debate and laughter among professors and graduate student attendees. Similar in size to the first *Weekly Seminar*, the auditorium was filled to capacity. For the last seminar of the semester, no research presentations are given. Instead, participants read announcements, give updates, and share and discuss research-related information.

"Welcome everyone," Broad squeaked, "to the last seminar of the semester."

Dowg, who was spread out in his chair reading, glanced up to see Broad on the microphone, rolled his eyes and went back to his paper.

"Let's begin with announcements and updates," Broad suggested, scanning the room for a raised hand to take the floor.

"Samuel."

The thick-framed leadership coach took the microphone. "My ability to chair or serve on any dissertation committees in the spring semester is tentative--my apologies--there are other matters competing for my time," Samuel said, shaking his head slightly as if to clear it of any annoyances. There were a few murmurs among the attendees, and then Broad reached for the microphone back.

"I would like to make early mention," Broad said after obtaining the floor from Samuel, "that in the spring semester, I will be conducting a reading of my recent work entitled *Neo-Marxism: Considerations for the New Age*. Room number, date and time forthcoming, I will..."

Metro had perked up at the mention of new age, but his thoughts were interrupted by a loud theatrical grunt. All eyes turned toward Dowg, whose head was slumped down onto his chest. He was snoring so loudly that asphyxiation seemed imminently near. Quickly, Metro stepped toward Dowg and nudged his shoulder.

"What?!" Dowg shouted before sitting up quickly in his chair, as if he had been jolted out of a relaxing rest into a state of sheer fear and terror at having fallen asleep on guard duty.

"Is there still the right to free speech?" Dowg rubbed his eyes, feigning alarm, as though he was unsure of how long he had been asleep or what Broad had convinced the audience to believe.

Dr. Spencer hid a smile, raised his hand, and stepped forward to take the microphone. "I would like to mention that the College of Veterinary Medicine and Biomedical Sciences at CSU was awarded a $2.3 million grant to study the neurobiology and reproductive physiology of animals in the CSU Veterinary Teaching Hospital. There are two graduate assistantships available and qualified applicants can apply in the spring semester – let me know if you might be interested and thank you for a great semester!"

Weekly Seminar attendees applauded, and Dr. Spencer held his hand up quickly and humbly before stepping towards his seat to sit down.

Roberta, envious of Spencer and the size of his grant, raised her hand and stepped forward, smiling pretentiously, to take the floor next. "UNC is currently working on two initiatives for the spring," Roberta announced. "We have opened discussion regarding the development of a major and minor in *Social Justice Studies*. Feel free to join our discussion group on developing a radical new curriculum.

We have partnered with the Criminology & Criminal Justice and Human Resources Departments at UNC to devise a potential graduate program that would culminate in a certificate for *Social Justice Investigation (SJI).*"

Dowg raised his hand, curious about what sort of jobs this degree would provide and whether or not cry rooms would be provided to the graduate students.

Roberta glanced past Dowg, skipped his raised hand, and went about her spiel.

"I'm even more pleased to be able to share my next news with you," she began pompously. "UNC is currently in the process, with guidance from Dr. Broad," she smiled smugly at him, "of forming a panel of experts to address student and faculty conduct that triggers or offends a member of our campus community. This panel will be called UNC's *Bias Response Team,* and we believe it will go a long way in protecting our students, staff and faculty from bias and hate. We are determined that UNC will be the epitome of safe space for all of our Bears and a shining example to all universities! Thank you!"

"Smells like an unconstitutional gulag tribunal to me, Robbie!" Dowg jumped to his feet, and posed, hands on hips, like a demented cheerleader. "So much for free speech at UNC!"

He readied himself into the starting pose of a cheer and began chanting:

Have no hate! Have no fear!
Robbie's *Bias Response Team* is here!"
Cookies! Crayons! Social Justice for all!
Let's write Fascist slogans on the wall!
For Radical Robbie is most expert of them all!"

Still in cheer mode, Dowg performed an athletic jump before dropping to one knee in front of Roberta and lauding her with enthusiastic jazz hands and his craziest clown smile.

Roberta tried to bore through him with her asymmetrical evil eye look. Dowg replied with a wink and an even wider grin, pointing his index fingers at his temples and twirling them to form the official academic nonverbal sign for *Batshit Crazy!*

Dowg ended his performance with a haphazard Nazi salute and clicked his heels together to stand at attention.

"Ja Wohl Meine Direktor!" Dowg goose stepped loudly and proudly back to his seat.

There was a moment of silence and then Dr. Schwede, who'd been absorbed in his tablet oblivious to Roberta's announcements and Dowg's one-man parade, looked up, realized the floor was now open and stepped forward. "First, I would like to congratulate Will and Aldo for jobs well done in our Department of Defense research," he said, motioning for them to stand for the room's applause.

"While we cannot make our findings known to the public for DOD reasons, we anticipate being awarded a $12 million grant from the Pentagon for continued development of our technologies in the Aerospace Engineering department at CU. We expect three graduate assistantships contingent on funding. I will keep you posted on developments." Schwede smiled before passing the microphone and then immediately returned to his tablet to solve yet another riddle of physics.

Ben's professor, Dr. Whitman, the chairperson of the College of Media, Communication, and Information, took the floor. You can see him there in the picture, top right, leaning on the column base, overseeing Ben, who is furiously scribbling away.

"We are pleased to be making progress in funding development involving a Center for Documentary and

Ethnographic Media. It is our hope to advance documentary practice through research, and we look forward to collaborating with other departments to these ends," Whitman announced to a round of applause and nodding heads.

Anthony sauntered towards the microphone and took the floor. "It was delightful to have practically every one of you up to Glen Haven for *Wednesday Night Services* this semester, and I hope you enjoyed yourselves and the hospitality. I'm already looking forward to the spring semester!" Attendees clapped loudly in appreciation for Anthony and his monthly suppers.

Dowg, who'd been quiet for more than he liked to be, rose from his seat. Roberta's head swiveled toward him in a partial panic but mostly in disgust when Dowg spoke. "Houndman and I would like to show our appreciation to Broad for hosting *Weekly Seminar* each semester and for being such a necessary and useful target for our verbal abuse." Everyone laughed, Houndman the most. Roberta relaxed slightly, glad to be outside of the crosshairs.

"We have a gift that reminds us of you Broad," Dowg said bending over to a bag on the floor next to his chair. Untying an easy knot made from the handles of a cloth grocery bag, he reached in with both hands and brought out a freshly and neatly plucked live chicken.

Broad looked at the bird without expression, despite the chuckles from the crowd. Dowg gently set the naked hen down and pointed her in Broad's general direction. The frightened chicken immediately ran across the auditorium towards a corner to slow, turn, and perform a nearly 270 degree glance at her surroundings. Calming down, she strutted toward Broad, stopped again, cocked her head and stared at him sideways for an abnormal amount of time as if scrutinizing the broad-shouldered, tiny-voiced professor.

The room was dead silent during the examination. Attendees watched the distinguished professor and the featherless biped stare at each other, both critically thinking, neither wanting to be the one to crack first. Suddenly the plucked chicken clucked loudly at Broad and sashayed back and forth in front of him, cackling and squawking, flapping her naked wings.

The auditorium suddenly filled with laughter. Will looked at Dowg and Houndman. Dowg was bent over, paralyzed with laughter, unable to even make a fist to wipe the tears from his eyes. Houndman looked worse off, holding his stomach and gasping for breath between booms of laughter.

Will noted that even Samuel was amused; his heavy shoulders bouncing with each deep chuckle at the barnyard humor.

As was customary, light refreshments were served at the last seminar of the semester, and the remainder of the time was devoted to open discussion among attendees. Broad and Spencer had not conversed since WNS in November in Glen Haven, so it was no accident that they picked up precisely where they had left off.

"There they go again," Houndman said grinning at Samuel and Halsey, "the little prick and the scientific giant. Watch your step--it could get thick."

Dowg, meanwhile, was trying to feed Broad's featherless chicken with crackers from the catered food, coaxing it closer for re-capture.

"For the sake of the common good," Broad said with his finger pointed skyward, "the state should be ruled by an intellectual elite that have no need for the consultation or approval of the ignorant masses. What is needed in this country is a form of government that protects the elite from the people so that the common good is not affected by the opinions and desires of the Beast or the demagogues." His voice was soft, his face unsmiling.

"I would agree that the masses seek profits more than honor and virtue, but if this just government of the elite is decision-making and acting outside of the public eye, how can anyone be assured that it is truthful? Or for the common good?" Spencer asked.

"Truth is not assured in a well-ordered state," Broad replied. "It is indeed necessary for the government to be able to lie to the people when it is in the best interests of the state, for the elite know best what is good."

Dowg guffawed, quickly forming a reply. "You're truly a totalitarian-loving elitist Broad; you love to talk the stuff of communist manifestos and other such Marxist gibberish-- that you're smart enough to run everyone's lives using corrupt institutions that pump government propaganda." Dowg watched as the naked chicken sidestepped closer to the cracker crumbs at his feet.

"It does beg the question," Spencer interjected, "How are rational citizens to be virtuous truth-seekers when they are not afforded the truth in matters that directly affect their lives?"

"Anything for the good of the state!" Dowg chided with sarcasm, "The bigger the government lie, the bigger the contribution to the common good!"

Dowg reached to grab the nude chicken. She struggled against his firm grasp and the inability to flap her featherless wings until she defecated on the floor. Upon completion of her bowel movement, the bird relaxed and calmly submitted to the dark safety of the cloth bag.

"Holy Shat, Broad!" Dowg said enthusiastically staring at the pile of chicken feces, "It's a sign! Hey, everyone! A form has been revealed to us this very day!"

Dowg tilted his head at various angles to look closer at the chicken shit for a more thorough examination of the purity of the turd's intended message.

"Any big plans to celebrate the birth of the baby jesus holiday?" Will asked Dowg with a sarcastically straight face. Homelessness was a new lifestyle for Will, and he was curious about what Dowg did between the fall and spring semesters, over the Christmas break.

"Oh Yes! Christmas is most certainly my favorite time of the year," Dowg stated with a wolfish grin. "Not only is it colder than Robbie's bitter heart, it's the season of consumerism madness fueled by unbridled selfish greed! All wrapped in a little-baby-in-a-manger-mythology of magically impregnated virgins and perfume-peddling star gazers! It's come to truly vex me as you may know."

"If that isn't enough," Dowg continued, "the sheeple will pray to some gawd over the holidays to ensure their health and then feast to the detriment of their health for days, usually starting the New Year feeling and looking fat, bloated and hungover." He shook his head disgustedly.

"To our health, great gawd all my dee!" Dowg proclaimed loudly, raising both hands skyward, a bottled water in his left hand, the index finger of his right hand pointed straight upward.

Chapter 27 – Finished Well

You know that in academia the best semester, the best class, the best exam or even the best dissertation or thesis is simply a finished one. The industry is about finishing, making clean breaks and moving on to new batches of empty buckets or unlit fires depending on your philosophy of higher education. Much depends on your philosophy actually, whether you know it or not or whether we discuss it or not. Regardless, you and I really should talk more about it, including how their fun-filled semester finally came to an end.

Mostly in defiance of the maddening consumption of the December holiday season, and partially due to the bitter cold, it was not uncommon for Dowg to travel over the winter break. On this particular occasion, he was on a bus headed to Los Angeles, California. He arrived in Grand Junction, Colorado for a change of buses and stepped off the metal coach into a mildly cold and snowless December morning.

Dowg sauntered into the Greyhound/Western Union Station eager to stretch his restless legs and determine his connecting bus. He glanced around the room to see a handful of travelers seated about the benches next to an inordinate number of snacks packed into large vending machines. Locating the newspapers, Dowg saw a fresh stack of loosely-bound copies of the day's **Denver Post**. Quickly slipping the top copy out, Dowg scurried to an empty bench and made himself comfortable by sprawling out for some rest and reading.

One the front page of the **Denver Post** was a large color picture of an enormously tall fire that had been taken during the dark of the night. Looking closer, he noted the outsized flames most resembled a gigantic fiery Roman candle fiercely penetrating the black firmaments with its defiant middle finger. Amused, Dowg read on.

At nearly the same time, Will was in his earthen den at Houndman's in Jamestown. He had built a warm fire and packed his belongings into the large duffle bag on the bed. The flashlight on the device held in his left hand cast a bright light onto the rock wall where Will inscribed with a chisel using his right hand:

Fuck Shit Up.

Yes, it's true, the young ADogs of action had buried their teeth firmly into the big ass of big gas and oil. Ben and Aldo had scouted the drill site days before and mapped the exact route the truck, loaded with explosives set by Halsey, would take. It was Will who hijacked the commissioner's truck from the security of the engineering center at CU using Dr. Schwede's office computers and software. As for Dowg, he had no idea what they had been planning, but judging by his howls of laughter in spite of the stares of the onlookers at the Greyhound Station, he seemed pleasantly tickled.

Since the authorities had no leads in the investigation of the massive wellhead explosion, I've pondered which of the 30 Tyrant Corporations they might chase down and maul next.

What do you think?

Will you listen to the Voice of Reason?

I hope that we can arrive at an answer fairly soon so that I can let the ADogs out to frolic some in the fresh air. In the outdoors, outside of any kennel or cage, and off any leash, where they can raise the howls and calls to *action-oriented shamelessness* against the dishonest institutions of your society. It's good exercise, keeps the rodent population thin; they could even tangle with some big cats, perhaps fuck some shit up.

Made in the USA
San Bernardino, CA
22 December 2018